Foreign Body

What if it happens to you?

To: Joan & Bill

Laurene

with lots of love and blessings

Laurene

H
HANSIB

WED 8 SEPT 2021

First published in Great Britain by Hansib Publications in 2021

P.O. Box 226, Hertford, SG14 3WY

info@hansibpublications.com
www.hansibpublications.com

Email: lotsofloveandblessings@btinternet.com
Website: www.lotsofloveandblessings.com

Cover design by Daniel Heijink
Email: danielheijink@gmail.com
Website: www.danheijink.com

ISBN 978-1-912662-36-4 (Paperback)
ISBN 978-1-912662-37-1 (Hardback)
ISBN 978-1-912662-38-8 (Kindle)
ISBN 978-1-912662-39-5 (ePub)

A CIP catalogue record for this book
is available from the British Library

Design & Production by Hansib Publications Ltd
Printed in Great Britain

IN MEMORY OF
Dr Bahaa Abdelmegid

Chapter One

She was startled by the very idea that she was to become a mother. How could this be? Marriage was to begin and end with her and him. No precautions were needed. Mumps had left her husband sterile, so she knew at the outset of their relationship that there would be no babies. Sitting in the waiting room, she was unable to comprehend the information. Eight months pregnant. What would Marcus say?

Marcia was a diminutive woman of twenty-eight, sweet-looking with blonde curls cascading down her shoulders. She was an only child and both her parents had died prior to her marriage. It was a simple encounter meeting Marcus. The weather had been hazy that morning when she stepped out of her car. She had been wearing a pink and grey suit, and, as she clutched her briefcase, her gloves fell to the ground in the car park. Rushing over, Marcus picked them up and handed them to her. She thanked him and they smiled at each other. The following morning, they met again and Marcus introduced himself. Their friendship deepened into a relationship, and within a year they were married.

Marcia had been feeling unwell for some time, but had put it down to the stress of her new job. It had been demanding, changing roles from junior to senior executive. Her weight gain was minimal and appeared to have been the benefit of the lunches and functions she was obliged to attend. Now, Marcia just sat there, staring into space, replaying in her head the words:

"Mrs Dos Santos, I am delighted to inform you that you are about eight to nine months pregnant. Congratulations!"

"But Dr Jameson ... it's impossible! Marcus cannot have children. We found out during our pre-nuptial health check that he was sterile. I couldn't possibly be pregnant!"

"Mrs Dos Santos, I am so sorry. Do forgive me, I did not mean to be insensitive, but I have to arrange an immediate scan as you have had no pre-natal checks. Would you mind waiting outside for a few minutes? I will be as quick as I can."

Dr Jameson ushered her into the waiting room. He had suppressed the urgency of the situation because he knew that Marcia was actually in labour.

* * *

Marcus was overseas on a business trip. What would she say to him? Should she tell him she was pregnant? Would he accuse her of infidelity? Should she wait until he came back? Questions, questions, questions flowed, but no answers came. She had been having abdominal pain during the previous night, and she was worried because she noticed her lingerie had been blood-stained. She had driven herself to the hospital. And now: this news.

Dr Jameson returned to find her clutching her abdomen with tears in her eyes. He now had a full-scale emergency on his hands. The arrival of the trolley to take her for the scan was opportune. With assistance, he helped her onto the trolley and, along with a nurse, accompanied her to the scanning room. A midwife and a nurse from the neonatal unit were summoned. There was no time to lose. Yet they did not make it to the delivery suite. As the scan was nearing completion, a baby boy arrived. Mother and baby were both screaming.

* * *

Who is going to tell Marcus? What would he say? The drugs and the pain caused Marcia to be mechanical in her thought-processes. Dr Jameson remained by her side throughout the birth. Later, taking down Marcus' contact details, he telephoned him.

"I am Dr Jameson of Somerville Memorial Hospital in London. Your wife asked me to call. She is here in the hospital, and although she is not seriously ill, we would request, as her next-of-kin, that you return as soon as it is convenient."

"Doctor, what is wrong with her?"

"Marcia came to us this morning feeling unwell. We completed some tests and we are going to do some more. Please tell me when to expect you and I will be there to greet you. Do try not to worry."

Dr Jameson could hear Marcus' breathing quicken and his voice start to shake.

"Please give me some information. This is shocking news. When I left this morning she was perfectly fine. What is wrong with her?"

"Marcia arrived at the emergency room alone, complaining of abdominal pain," the doctor continued. "We have carried out some initial tests and we – as I said – we have to complete the analysis. She is conscious and is asking for you. At present, the nurses are with her and she is being monitored closely."

"Is Marcia all right?" Marcus interjected, his voice full of fear. "Will she be all right? I am scared by this sudden news. Please tell me that Marcia is all right."

Dr Jameson adopted his most soothing voice.

"As I said, we are monitoring Marcia and keeping a close eye on her. We are doing all we can. Please be assured that your wife is having the best of care. She does not appear to be in any immediate danger, she is conscious and she keeps asking for you. Will you be able to return soon?"

"Yes, Doctor," said Marcus. "I will be there as soon as I can get on a plane."

"Good. Please keep me informed of your travel plans, and I will see you directly on your arrival at the hospital. I will also keep Marcia informed."

"Thank you, Doctor," said Marcus, gratefully. "Please look after Marcia for me. I love her so much. I can't afford to lose her."

"Try not to worry," Dr Jameson repeated. "Marcia is in the best place and we are taking good care of her. She will be happy when I tell her that you are returning soon."

"Thank you Doctor. Thank you."

Once the call was over, Dr Jameson sighed deeply. As he walked back to Marcia's room to give her the news, he reflected on what he had told Marcus. It had been a close call. He had made a conscious decision not to tell him about the baby, as he was aware of Marcus' medical problem, and did not wish to alarm him with the wholly unexpected news that he was now a father.

* * *

Marcus caught the first plane out of New York. His mission, which was to procure an important contract for his company, seemed no longer possible or important. The telephone call from the doctor had preoccupied him. He knew he had to get back to London immediately. He and Marcia had been married for five years, and he loved her with an intensity that sometimes frightened him.

Daybreak came a few hours after Marcus' arrival in London. The faint sunlight dazzled through the morning mist as he made his way from the airport to the hospital by taxi.

"Please, God," he prayed, "I cannot live without her."

Just ten hours after the telephone call from Dr Jameson, Marcus was sitting in the doctor's office, asking to see Marcia.

"Mr Dos Santos, your wife is well, and, though apprehensive, is looking forward to seeing you."

Marcus gave a huge intake of breath.

"What is wrong with her? If she is well, why did you call me? My business in New York was of immense importance. Is this some kind of joke?"

The doctor paused, and then smiled broadly.

"No Marcus. This is not a joke. In fact, congratulations are in order because your wife has a beautiful baby boy ..."

Marcus was stunned by the unexpected news, and stared at the doctor with a look of disbelief on his face.

"What! She is pregnant? She has a son?" He paused. "It can't be. We can't have children. I can't make babies... Are you sure that it is Marcia, my wife, who has a baby?"

All his pent-up emotions came to the fore, and Marcus burst into tears.

"What am I going to do?" he cried.

Dr Jameson remained silent for a while, then quietly said, "Shall I take you to see your wife and baby? She is in a private room."

Marcus was still in a state of shock.

"My baby!" he repeated. "But I can't make babies! I have a baby? Are you certain it is Marcia who has a baby?"

Marcus got to his feet and paced up and down the doctor's office. His hands jittered as he attempted to control his feelings. He seemed unable to comprehend the enormity of the conversation. All of his life, doctors had told him that he would never be a father. Yet here he was, in Dr Jameson's office, as the father of a new-born son. Quickly, he sat down again as his legs began to fail him.

"Doctor, are you absolutely certain that Marcia has had a baby?" Marcus asked.

"Yes. Absolutely certain. I delivered the baby myself," Dr Jameson responded.

Marcus appeared to struggle as he endeavoured to collect his thoughts. The doctor quietly repeated the question.

"Would you like to see your wife and son? She has been asking for you. She has not had any visitors so far, and quite frankly, is as shocked as you are. Of course, she never expected to be pregnant, and within an hour of being told the news, the baby was born. I saw her myself, and was just completing the foetal scan when the child arrived. Your wife was frightened and tearful, but the nurses have been looking after her. There are three things she needs at this time: kindness, love and you. We will be able to deal with any medical questions later."

"All right. All right. Take me to see Marcia. I need to be with her," Marcus said, with a sigh of resignation.

Marcus remained silent as Dr Jameson accompanied him to Marcia's room, where they were ushered into a cubicle by a nurse. Marcia was asleep. In a small cot beside her was a bundle of blue bed-clothes, and Marcus could see a crop of black curls. He walked over and gazed at the baby.

He was a father. Of course, he had never expected to be a father, but the baby lying asleep in the cot was definitely his. Gently, he reached for the infant's hand and the baby's fingers curled around his own. A rush of emotions engulfed him, and in an instant he felt a wave of pure love for his wife and son. Tears welled in his eyes, for he had missed an important time. Moving over to the bed, he leaned over, and covered his sleeping wife with kisses. Marcia awoke with a start. As he embraced her, Marcus told her how much he loved her and reassured her that they would be able to cope with their unexpected arrival.

Marcia looked at her husband sleepily.

"Don't you have any doubts?" she said. "I didn't know I was pregnant. I came to the hospital with abdominal pain, and then the baby arrived."

Marcus looked at her and laughed nervously.

"Shh, shh, it's all right," he said. "We have been given a miracle. He looks just like me when I was born: a mop of black curls and a wrinkled face."

He smiled broadly.

"I am so happy to be a father. When Mama finds out, she will be overjoyed to have a grandson that she never thought possible."

Marcia shuddered inwardly as she thought of her mother-in-law's indifference towards her.

"I hope Mama will be happy," Marcia murmured.

To give the new family some time alone, Dr Jameson and the nurse slipped quietly out of the room. They were unaware of the hostilities that would ensue because of the mysterious circumstances of the baby's birth.

Chapter Two

The happy couple were thrilled to be taking their unexpected arrival home. Marcus was proudest of all. He had a son. He never knew he would ever have a child, let alone a son. He was ecstatic, with his face bearing a permanent smile. He kept repeating: "I am a father. I am a father." This repetitive phrase amused Marcia.

"Wait until we tell Mama. I hope the news will make her happy," Marcia said unconvincingly.

On the way home, Marcia sat in the back of the car with the baby. He was asleep, and Marcus kept asking her if the infant was all right.

"Yes. He is asleep. That is what babies do." She laughed. "I am listening to his heart beating and watching the rise and fall of the blanket as he breathes. He is so tiny. And so very precious... He feels so warm and he is beautiful."

"I can't wait to get home and call Mama and Auntie Magdalena," Marcus said. "It is a shame that Claudia is staying with them at the moment, otherwise I am certain that she would have been here with us now."

Marcia smiled. She knew how much Marcus adored his sister, and also how kind Claudia had been to her the first time they had met.

"I am excited, but also unsure." Marcia frowned. "It will be such a shock for them. It was traumatic for me to be told I was pregnant, and then within an hour to have a baby. I was terrified. I just wanted to be with you." Her eyes filled with tears as she remembered.

Marcus felt an inward rush of guilt because he had not been there to support his wife in her time of need.

"I am here now, and together we have a beautiful baby boy," he said. "Mama will be so happy. I think we should name him after Papa. What do you think?"

Marcia agreed, as she always did.

"That is wonderful," she said. "Naming the baby after Papa is sure to make Mama even happier. She misses her husband so much."

Smiling, Marcia felt relaxed. She was genuinely happy that the baby would bear the name of her late father-in-law, but inwardly wondered how her husband's mother would accept the news about the unexpected arrival of the baby.

* * *

As soon as they arrived at the flat, Marcus telephoned his mother.

"Mama! I am so excited," he shouted down the phone. "I am a father. I am the happiest of men.

Marcia had a baby boy and he looks just like me when I was born."

There was silence, then a sharp intake of breath.

"What do you mean?" his mother replied icily. "You are a father? You can't..."

"But Mama," Marcus interrupted. "Marcia has given birth to a beautiful baby boy." Marcus repeated, "He looks just like me when I was born, with a mop of black curly hair."

His mother laughed sarcastically.

"Has she fooled you?" she said. "You know you can't have children."

"But Mama, listen," Marcus pleaded. "We are going to name him after Papa."

"How dare you! Don't you name that child after Papa," his mother screeched. "How can you be sure it's your baby? You know you can't have children."

Marcus was taken aback by this outburst and was shocked into silence. His mother had always doted on him, and he thought that she was fond of Marcia.

"I have never trusted that girl," she added contemptuously.

Marcus adopted a conciliatory tone.

"Mama, please don't say such harsh things about Marcia," he said. "I love her and she loves me. She would never be unfaithful to me."

"You men," she laughed sarcastically. "You are all the same, far too trusting. We will see. We will see."

As she repeated the words a second time, there was a note in his mother's voice that Marcus did not understand.

"Mama," he said. "What do you mean? You can't speak about my wife like that!"

"I can indeed," she responded. "Marcus, you know you cannot have children. That girl has fooled you. I have never trusted her"

"Mama, how could you be so cruel?" Marcus replied angrily. "Why do you hate Marcia and why do you say such terrible things about her?"

"Don't mention her name to me. She has tricked you and I am going to find out who is the father of that child. She has brought shame to our family name."

"Mama. Stop it. Stop it now!" Marcus shouted.

"You fool. You stupid fool. You know that you can't have children and yet you believe this girl instead of me. You stupid fool."

Marcus became quite angry but spoke in measured tone.

"Mama, if you are going to be unkind to Marcia, I am ending this conversation now. Marcia has just had our baby, your grandson. If you wish to accept him, that's fine but please Mama, don't insult my wife and me. The baby belongs to Marcia and me."

"We will soon see about that. You can't have babies. That girl has tricked you."

Marcus hung up. He stood trembling in the hallway. He stared at the phone. The joy he felt drained from him, leaving him troubled and frightened by his mother's reaction to the news about the birth. Marcia called out from the bedroom.

"Marcus, Marcus, you were shouting. What did Mama say? When will she come to see her grandson?"

Marcus entered the room, his head bowed. He looked at Marcia with tears in his eyes and replied in a controlled voice.

"She said... well... Marcia, she accused you of infidelity."

Marcia, visibly shocked by this revelation, cried out.

"Me? Why would she say that? Why? I don't understand."

"I don't know. Mama was very angry. I am confused. I thought she would be happy for us. I don't understand. I just don't understand." Marcus shook his head from side to side.

"Marcus. You are frightening me. Do you believe we have a son or do you believe that I have a son? How can Mama be so cruel? Please say it is not true, Marcus."

"Marcia, please. That baby is our baby. You and I are the parents of that baby. I love you Marcia. I knew from the first moment I saw you that I loved you, and when you dropped your eyes when you caught me looking at you, I knew that you loved me too."

Marcus walked over to the bed and embraced his wife as she began to weep.

Through her tears she said, "But Mama. Mama must hate me now. Why would she be so cruel about me? Why?"

"Don't you worry about Mama. I will deal with her. While I was talking to Dr Jameson, he asked me if I wanted a sperm count as I hadn't had one for five years. He also offered me a DNA test. I declined because I know that the baby is ours. Marcia, that is the amount of trust I have in you and in our relationship. It never crossed my mind that you could be unfaithful to me. I have never doubted you and I will never doubt you. Marcia, I love you."

"Marcus, I love you. I was so frightened when I went to the hospital and you were not with me."

Marcus continued, "Since Papa died, Mama has become very possessive towards me. I think the shock of my becoming a father was difficult for her. It caused her to say the things that she said, so please Marcia, don't be too hard on her. She will come around. You will see. I will get Claudia to speak to Mama. Everything will be alright."

"Oh Marcus, I love you so much, thank you for loving me and believing in me. At least Claudia will be happy to be an auntie."

* * *

Two days later, Marcus opened his front door. He was surprised to see his mother, sister, aunt, and twin cousins standing in the entrance. His mother and aunt rushed through the door. Marcus held the door open for his sister and cousins.

"Where is this baby?" his mother shouted.

"Don't you want to ask about Marcia? She is in bed, holding our baby. She has just finished feeding him and he is drifting off to sleep."

"We have to look at that baby and speak to Marcia," his mother screeched. "She tricked you. That girl has tricked you. You can't have babies. We are here to see the baby and question Marcia."

His aunt and mother pushed past him and entered the bedroom without the courtesy of a knock. They looked at Marcia.

"Marcia, let us see that baby!" Mama said angrily.

"Hello Mama, hello Auntie," said Marcia, smiling. "How are you both?"

Mama was incandescent with rage.

"Never mind us", she half-shouted. "We are here to see the baby. We have to look at him." She fixed her daughter-in-law with a steely gaze. "You must remember that my son can't have babies. You have tricked him. Tell me now - who is the real father of this baby!"

As Auntie nodded in agreement, Marcia erupted into tears. Shaking with fright, she clutched her son closer to her. At that point, Marcus entered the room. Rushing over to the bed, he lifted the baby from Marcia's arms and cradled him. Marcia took the bedsheets and covered her head with them in a desperate attempt at self-preservation.

With his face contorted with rage, Marcus turned to his mother.

"Mama, don't you dare touch my baby," he said firmly. "You arrived less than a minute ago with all the family that you could muster. And in just that short time, you have managed to insult my wife and me in the deepest possible way. You have accused Marcia of infidelity and now she is in tears. For goodness sake, she has just had a baby. That baby is my own baby. You have no right to treat her in that way."

Mama was unmoved.

"Huh," she cackled, knowingly. "We have to look at that baby."

She looked at her son with a look of pity, the venom still dripping from her lips. "You fool," she repeated. "You cannot have babies. Countless doctors have told you that. And you yourself know that too."

She raised her voice again to screech at her daughter-in-law.

"Marcia, who is the father of this baby?" she shouted as she pointed to the baby in Marcus' arms.

Marcia remained silent, her face hidden under the bedclothes.

Marcus decided to try a new tactic.

"But Mama, look at this baby," he said, his tone mellowing slightly. "He has a mop of black curls, just like I do."

Mama tutted loudly. "All babies look alike," she said scornfully. "Look at Andreas," she said, grabbing her nephew by the arm and turning him to face Marcus.

"Look at him. Look at him," Mama screamed. "He is my sister's, your aunt's son and he is a redhead. Felix, his twin, has black hair."

Andreas stared at the floor, feeling embarrassed, while Marcus responded.

"And what is that supposed to mean, Mama?"

His mother paused, and then pursed her lips.

"A mop of black curls means nothing," she said acidly.

The baby began to cry.

With his face contorted with rage, Marcus could feel the anger rising in his voice.

"Mama, Auntie," he half-shouted. "I think you had better leave. Get out. Just leave my wife, our son, and me alone. Get out of my house. Go."

An almost imperceptible smile graced Mama's lips.

"We are not going anywhere until you see some sense," she said, her voice lowering. "My dear son, you remember that between the age of thirteen and twenty-two, you were tested every single year without fail. The doctors said that you would never, ever, be able to father a child. You need sperm to have babies."

The venom returned to her voice, and she gestured towards Marcia.

"She has tricked you," she stated triumphantly. "Can't you see? That baby is not yours."

"How could you say these things?" Marcus said, his tone firm. "How could you be so cruel to Marcia and me? Mama, it's a miracle. Marcia and I have a son, with a mop of black curls just like mine." He paused. "You and Auntie are being too aggressive," he added firmly. "Look, you are making Marcia ill. She has only just given birth and she has no need to be treated like this by you."

Sobbing and shaking, Marcia pulled the bedsheet off her face. Marcus passed the crying baby to her, and then turned to his mother and aunt.

"Leave. Leave now. Get out," he said. "Look at what you have done to my wife. She is a nervous wreck. I have never seen her like this. I will have to call the doctor. She is in a very fragile state indeed. Just leave now."

His sister Claudia stepped forward. Until now, she had been silent.

"Marcus," she said carefully, "may I hold the baby, please?"

Marcus stared at his sister,

"Not before you say hello to Marcia," he said, "and only if you are polite to her, too."

Claudia was shocked by her brother's statement.

"Oh. Oh. Oh. I have never been rude to Marcia," she said. "You know how much I love her, I really do. And I certainly don't agree with Mama and Auntie and whatever they are saying. I am quite shocked by Mama's behaviour."

Turning to her sister-in-law, Claudia went over to the bed and placed her hand on Marcia's arm.

"Congratulations Marcia," she half-whispered, smiling. "You have made me an Aunt. I never expected to be one. May I please hold my nephew?"

In a louder voice, she added as she winked at Marcia, "I think it is wonderful to have a baby, whoever it belongs to."

Claudia leaned over the bed and hugged Marcia, brushing the tears from her face. Marcia passed the infant to Claudia, who cradled him lovingly in her arms.

Mama's face was a picture of hatred.

"This is despicable," she snapped. "You have all been conned by that awful girl. I have never liked her."

Taking Auntie by the arm, Mama and her sister stormed out of the room. A few seconds later, the sound of the front door slamming reverberated around the flat.

There was a tense silence. Marcus and his cousins looked at each other, before Andreas finally broke the silence.

"It's difficult for us to go against our mother and our aunt," he said. "Claudia was very brave to say what she said in front of them but she is older than we are. We are happy for both of you. Marcia has always been kind to us and we love her very much."

Andreas paused, as though weighing up a difficult decision.

"We think we have to go now with Mama and Auntie, before they cause any more distress to Marcia," he said.

"Can we kiss the baby please?" added Felix.

Marcus drew closer to his cousins and embraced them. Claudia came over and the twins kissed the baby's forehead. They smiled and said to Marcus playfully, "He looks just like you."

The twins then went over to the bed, hugged and kissed Marcia's tear-stained face and gave her their congratulations on the birth of the baby.

"Are you coming Claudia?" Andreas asked, as they stood by the bedroom door.

"No," she said. "I am staying right here. I need to help Marcia and enjoy being an aunt."

With that, Andreas and Felix said their goodbyes and left the flat. It was just the four of them now.

Marcia, her face riddled with tearful apologies, turned to her sister-in-law and said, "I am so sorry to cause this friction in your family."

"Don't apologise," Claudia said soothingly. "You haven't done anything wrong. Take no notice of them. That is how they behave when they are not in control. They like to have everything their way."

Claudia smiled, before continuing.

"I am happy to be an aunt. Can I stay here and help you? I just don't want to return to the hotel and listen to them and their toxic speculation about who is the father of the baby. They know that it is Marcus' baby. And even if the child didn't have a mop of black curly hair, you can tell by looking at you and Marcus that the baby is Marcus' son."

For the first time, Marcia smiled through her tears. She had become frightened by the vitriolic abuse that she had suffered from her mother-in-law. She had had no idea that his mother hated her with such venom. It was true, sometimes she had felt uncomfortable when alone with Mama, but she never imagined that Mama had such feelings of hatred towards her. With his sister, though, things were different, and she had always felt safe whenever Claudia was present.

Marcus went over to wife, and hugged and kissed her.

"I don't know why Mama said such hurtful things," he said. "Don't worry. Everything will be all right. We have a beautiful baby. You have made me a father and I am so very, very happy." He smoothed his wife's hair and caressed her tear-stained face.

"I love you, I always have and I always will. Just get some rest and Claudia and I will look after the baby."

"Thank you," said Marcia. "Thank you. Yes, I must rest now because the baby needs feeding every two hours. My milk flow is erratic, so the nurse advised regular feeding to ensure that he gets enough nourishment. I am very tired, exhausted even."

She turned to her sister-in-law.

"Thank you. Claudia," she said. "Thank you for your support. I really do appreciate it. It will be great to have your help. I feel so tired all of the time."

* * *

Claudia and Marcus withdrew into the sitting room, with Claudia holding the sleeping baby in her arms. They sat down in silence. Marcus was happy to see Claudia rocking the baby. He felt relieved to have the support of his sister. A postdoctoral research associate in comparative genetics, Claudia was twenty-nine, a year older than Marcus and Marcia. Marcus always had the support of his sister. He recalled how, when he developed mumps at the age of thirteen, she had devoted her time to him on his return from hospital. His adolescent years were spent with yearly visits to hospital to check his sperm count, as mumps can result in pubescent males presenting with infertility. Claudia used to tease him every year when their mother took him to the hospital for tests. When she went to university to study medicine she told Marcus that it was her aim to find a way to make him become a father so that she could be an aunt.

Marcus slipped out of the room and returned to the bedroom. His wife was asleep. He stood in the doorway observing her for a time. The half-light in the room emphasised his angular features. He was tall, dark and his usual appearance was of a Catalan movie star. Now, he looked gaunt and unsure of himself. He was unprepared for the vituperative outburst by his mother and the agreement by his aunt. He always thought that he had a wonderful family. When he met Marcia, his mother appeared to accept her. She told him, "If she will marry you knowing that you are unable to have children, then she can't be all that bad."

At that time he laughed and thought nothing of it. Now, he wondered at her words. They haunted him. He felt an overwhelming degree of sadness. He must not cry. He had to be strong for Marcia and the baby. He composed himself and returned to the drawing room. Claudia was lying on the sofa cradling the sleeping baby in her arms. She appeared asleep but stirred when he entered the room. After a while she handed the baby to Marcus.

"I have to return to my flat to collect some things but I will be back tomorrow after I speak with my boss."

"Will you go to the hotel to see Mama?" asked Marcus.

"No. I will speak to her another time. Now is not a good time. She is too angry," replied Claudia.

"You are right. I don't know what overcame her. I always knew that she resented Marcia but I thought it was because she did not have Papa anymore." Marcus sighed.

"I will talk to her, but you, Marcia and the baby are my priority now. Will you be all right until I return?" Claudia asked.

"Yes. I am glad you are back. I will call you if we need help," Marcus responded.

"Say goodbye to Marcia for me. Tell her to call me in the night if she needs help. Bye."

Claudia kissed the baby's forehead and said goodbye to Marcus. He then placed the sleeping baby in his cot. Marcia was still asleep. He returned to the drawing room and sat down. He cast his eyes on the pictures of his family that adorned the oak-panelled walls of the room. Most were his wedding photos with Marcia, his family and their guests. It was a spacious room decorated in neutral colours. A vase of tropical flowers stood on the mantelpiece. They were a special gift from Marcus to welcome Marcia and the baby home. He had chosen the floral arrangement, as they were Marcia's mother's favourite.

Marcus thought about Papa. If only he was still alive to welcome his grandson. He wondered at his mother's behaviour. He had no idea why she behaved in that unseemly manner. An image of his father stared at him from the photograph on the mantelpiece. He resolved to name the baby Marcus Aurelius after his father.

Chapter Three

After leaving the flat, Mama, her sister and the boys returned to their hotel. Mama paced up and down the room attempting to control her rage. They had arrived by air from Andorra and she was angry at what she felt was a betrayal. In truth she had been angry ever since Marcus had telephoned about the baby. Every time her sister attempted to speak, Maria's behaviour became irrational.

Magdalena sat on the bed looking at her sister, and said, "Please Maria. Can we at least talk about what is bothering you? The twins are finding the atmosphere unsettling. Perhaps we were a bit insensitive. After all, Marcia just had a baby."

Maria was wrapped up in her own thoughts and was not listening to her sister.

"You know Magdalena, how can Marcus behave in this way? My son, my only son takes sides with that girl. How could he? How could he speak to his Mama like that? If only my husband were still alive I am certain that Marcus would not be so disrespectful to me."

"But Maria, he has to take sides with Marcia…"

"Don't mention her name in this house. That girl has tricked my son and brought shame on the family."

Magdalena continued but Maria was not really listening. She was caught up in her own anger.

"She is his wife and she was present, he could hardly not agree with her."

"And Claudia too. My own daughter," Maria continued, speaking to herself.

"Claudia and Marcia were always friends ever since Marcus brought her home. She was happy to gain a sister. Don't be too upset with her. Maybe we were a bit harsh towards Marcia when she just had a baby. We should have waited," Magdalena said, in an attempt to placate Maria.

Maria's anger spilt over in tears.

"How could you accuse me? I am his mother. That girl has deceived us. I just know. A mother always knows the truth."

Magdalena stood up and put her arms around her sister and said, "Please don't cry. It's a shock for all of us. Especially you. It's so unexpected."

Andreas and Felix, the twins, spoke simultaneously.

"Please don't cry Auntie Maria. It will be all right. You will see."

Chapter Four

Marcus awoke in the night to the sound of his baby crying. He got out of bed. He lifted the baby from his cot. He took him over to Marcia. He called to her. She did not respond. He touched her. Her skin was hot. She mumbled to him. Still holding the crying baby, he rushed to the phone and dialled emergency. Something was wrong. Something was dreadfully wrong.

The paramedics' arrival was almost immediate. They began to treat Marcia. They took the family to the hospital. Marcus was relieved of the baby by a nurse who took him to the baby unit. Marcus stood outside the Emergency Room. Confused. He was not certain of anything. He was on his own. Claudia had returned to her flat to collect essentials for her stay with Marcia prior to returning to work to speak to her boss.

Marcus paced backwards and forwards along the bleak corridor. Movement in and out of the unit where Marcia was being treated left him bewildered. No one spoke to him. He was unable to comprehend the events that were taking place. A few days previously his life was settled, now it was in turmoil. Mama's behaviour was incomprehensible. He did not want to think about it. Marcia's illness troubled him but he did not want to think about that either. In truth, he did not want to think of anything.

Distracted for a moment, he focused on the drab grey walls. Their dullness was interrupted by a few nondescript paintings. They were different coloured lines painted at angles that seemed kindergarten in nature. He wondered whether that area was the genesis of the paintings. He desperately tried to occupy his mind with anything but his wife's illness. He thought of calling Claudia – she always knew what to do – but he was too apprehensive. Hospital staff kept going in and out of the room where Marcia had been taken. No one spoke to him. He felt unsure of himself.

After what seemed like an eternity, Dr Jameson arrived. He greeted Marcus. Marcus was happy to see a friendly face.

"I am sorry to learn that Marcia has taken ill. As soon as I am made aware I will have a word with you about her condition."

"Thank you Doctor. I am worried as no one has spoken to me."

"I will send someone to stay with you but I have to go into the Emergency Room now. I need to find out what is causing Marcia's illness. As soon as I am able I will return and let you know."

It was an hour later when he emerged. He took Marcus into the relatives' room. They sat down. His demeanour was grave. He observed Marcus face. It was desperate with hope that his wife could be saved but reflected the fear that Dr Jameson might not be able to save her. Dr Jameson felt unsure how to respond to Marcus' feelings of utter desolation. It is a rare occurrence to have a maternal death, and as he spoke to Marcus he knew there was a real possibility in this case. When he spoke his voice was soothing and he chose his words carefully.

"Your wife is very seriously ill. She has sepsis. It is a condition where harmful bacteria release their toxins into a wound creating an infection. We suspect that it is a post-delivery infection and we have commenced treatment with intravenous broad-spectrum antibiotics. We have already isolated your baby and we have started prophylactic treatment with antibiotics as a precaution. He has been fed and the nurses are looking after him. Our immediate concern is for your wife. We are monitoring her closely, but we have to wait before we can anticipate the outcome. It was good that the paramedics got to her while she was still conscious. It gives us hope."

Marcus sat there. He rested his head in his hands. His face strained. He could not look at Dr Jameson. He listened. He knew about Toxic Shock Syndrome. A former colleague at his previous job had died from it. It was because she was allergic to the tampon that she had used, a brand that she had not used before. Marcia had just had her baby. The hospital had given her special feminine hygiene pads to use. She had no reason to use tampons. Through trembling lips, he said to Dr Jameson, "Marcia was not using any tampons. She had no need."

Dr Jameson got up and rested his hand on Marcus' shoulders. "Toxic Shock Syndrome has several causes. Marcia may have picked up the infection post-delivery. It is too early to say. I am sorry for your distress. I will keep you informed of developments and I will arrange a room at the hospital so you can stay near your wife. Is there anyone I can call for you?"

Marcus thought of his sister again. He told Dr Jameson that Claudia had left that afternoon to return to her work. She was going to speak to her boss to request some time off so she could help Marcus and Marcia with the baby. Marcus gave Claudia's details to Dr Jameson and the details of her boss, Dr Kate Smith.

"Marcus, we have administered emergency treatment to your wife and son but for us to continue we need next of kin and parental consent for your wife and son."

"Yes. Of course."

After completing the documents Dr Jameson withdrew to his office. Marcus returned to the chair in the waiting room and buried his head in his hands.

* * *

Morning came quickly. Dr Jameson sat at his desk and proceeded to make all the arrangements. He called Claudia's boss and apprised her of the situation. It turned out that Dr Jameson knew Kate. They had studied medicine together. Smith was a name that he did not recognise as it was her married name. He was happy to renew her acquaintance.

Dr Jameson returned to the waiting room. Marcus was still sitting in the chair asleep. He entered the Emergency Room then returned and took Marcus to see his wife. Marcia was in an induced coma. The various paraphernalia of artificial ventilation was explained to him. He was introduced to a named nurse who would be responsible for looking after Marcia when she was eventually transferred to the intensive care unit.

Marcus spent the rest of the day sitting beside Marcia, holding her hand and pleading with her to stay with him, letting her know how much he loved her. He talked to her about the baby but soon he was overcome with exhaustion and fell asleep in the chair.

* * *

Claudia arrived later in the day. Marcus was relieved to see her. She hugged him close. He was bereft and Claudia did her best to console him. They both went to see the baby and discovered he showed no signs of infection. He was being monitored. The staff were pleased that they had little Marcus Aurelius to look after and that he remained healthy. Marcus returned to Marcia's room. Claudia accompanied him.

He sat down by the bedside and Claudia stood observing Marcia. The hum of the ventilator and the beep of the heart monitor created an eerie sound in an otherwise silent room. Dr Jameson arrived a few minutes later.

"Good evening Marcus. And you must be Claudia," he said, extending his hand in greeting. "I am pleased that you were able to be here to support Marcus and Marcia."

"Pleased to meet you, Dr Jameson. Thank you again for the telephone call. Kate was delighted to renew your acquaintance. Can Marcus and I discuss Marcia's condition with you? He tells me that you have been supportive."

Dr Jameson took them into his office and they sat down.

"Marcus, your wife has puerperal fever. In layman's terms, it is called childbed fever. It can occur after the first twenty-four hours of childbirth and up to about fourteen days post-delivery. As I told you previously, the cause is a bacterial infection and we are treating it but I have to say shock can play havoc with one's immune system. I know the baby's arrival was a shock, but, is there anything else bothering Marcia? She seemed contented when she left hospital with you."

Marcus looked at Claudia and shook his head. Tears streamed down his face. Claudia went over to her brother and held his hand. She looked directly at the doctor.

"Dr Jameson, two days after Marcia was discharged from hospital, our mother arrived. She accused Marcia of infidelity, and of fooling Marcus into thinking it was his baby when she had been having an affair. Marcia was in bed at the time and was very frightened by my mother's and my aunt's outburst. I suppose that can be construed as additional shock."

It was a while before Dr Jameson spoke. He was digesting what Claudia had said. Marcus said nothing. When Dr Jameson spoke he chose his words carefully.

"Marcus, do you believe that Marcus Aurelius is your baby?"

"I have no doubt that the baby is mine," replied Marcus.

"Claudia, how about you?" Dr Jameson requested.

Claudia responded without hesitating. "Dr Jameson, Marcia loves my brother and when they are together it is amazing how well-suited they are to each other. Marcia would never be unfaithful to Marcus. She is besotted with him and he with her. Mama and Auntie were very cruel to her. That is why I wanted to stay to support her."

Dr Jameson said, "Marcia has experienced a cryptic pregnancy. This is a medical phenomenon where one is unaware that one is pregnant until the birth. The sudden appearance of the baby can lead to major emotional issues for both parents. Marcus, in your case, all your life you have been told you are sterile and then a baby arrives. In addition to this, your wife is seriously ill, so, I suspect that you are unable to maintain rational thoughts. It is commendable that your sister is supporting you as her knowledge of genetics will help to alleviate much of your fears."

"Doctor, I have no doubt that Marcus Aurelius is my baby. What troubles me is my mother's behaviour towards Marcia. It has affected me so much that I am unable to control my emotions. I love my wife and I love my mother, now I am faced with having to choose between the two."

Dr Jameson looked at them both and said, "Would you allow me to do DNA testing on you, Marcia and the baby, plus other tests on you, Marcus, to establish once and for all what you already know? It would help your mother to accept the baby and mend the rift that she has created."

Marcus looked at Claudia and nodded.

Claudia responded by saying, "We are a close family and my mother will not speak to me because I support Marcia, so I think it will help if Marcus agrees."

Dr Jameson said, "And what about Marcia? She is unable to decide at present, so Marcus has to decide for her."

Marcus looked at Dr Jameson and said, "Yes. Doctor, I agree with my sister. Do whatever you need to do. I just want my family back the way we were before. Please make Marcia well again. I love her so much. I can't live without her."

"Thank you, Marcus. The team looking after Marcia needs to keep an eye on her in the induced coma for at least another twenty-four hours. She does not appear to have any major organ damage but we have to be cautious. Try not to worry. You have my private number, you can call me anytime."

Claudia turned to the doctor and said, "We are grateful to you, Dr Jameson, and I am especially indebted to you for arranging the time off with my boss so I can be here for Marcia, Marcus and the baby."

* * *

Marcus and Claudia emerged from the doctor's office and returned to Marcia's room. Marcus walked towards the bed, observing the rise and fall of the ventilator that was maintaining his wife's life. He sat down and reached for her hand.

He leant over and whispered, "I love you Marcia. Please remember how much you mean to me and Marcus Aurelius."

The only response was the beep, beep, beep of the monitors. Claudia asked the nurse if she could look at Marcia's charts and the nurse gave Claudia permission. She studied the charts while Marcus continued holding Marcia's hand and telling her the baby was well and being spoilt by the nurses on the baby unit. He urged her to get well soon as he and the baby missed her and needed her back. Marcus sensed that his hand was being squeezed. It was feeble, so he thought maybe he imagined it.

* * *

The following morning, Marcus went to the phlebotomist to have blood and various other samples taken. Samples were also taken from Marcia, Claudia and the baby. Claudia spent some time in the baby unit with Marcus Aurelius. She was allowed to hold, change and feed him. He was a contented baby and seemed to spend a lot of the time sleeping. She was becoming comfortable in her role as an aunt.

Later that morning, the medical team arrived to assess Marcia. Claudia and Marcus waited outside the room while the team busied themselves with their assessments and discussions. Marcia's overnight observations were stable and the decision was taken to wean her off artificial ventilation.

Claudia and Marcus were then informed of the team's decision, which was to commence later in the day after the morning test results became available. Marcus became agitated. He tugged at his clothes, his mouth began to twitch and his eyes began to flutter. Claudia moved towards him and embraced him. He began to sob uncontrollably. She took him to his room and told him to get some rest. He lay on the bed and succumbed to sleep.

Claudia returned to the intensive care unit to find that Marcia was no longer attached to the ventilator. Instead she had a manual oral airway inserted and was receiving oxygen via a mask, as she was still suffering the residual effects of the drugs used for artificial ventilation compliance. She appeared to be asleep. Claudia sat down by the bedside and held Marcia's hand. She told her that the baby was healthy and had not contracted any infection. She also told her that Marcus had stayed with her all the time but that she had sent him to bed to get some rest. Marcia coughed and expelled her airway. The nurse hurried over to her side.

"Hi Marcia. How are you feeling? You have been asleep for a while."

Marcia tried to speak. She brought her hand up to her throat. She looked at the nurse, and then looked at Claudia. Her eyes were moist with tears. Claudia held her hand and she squeezed it. The nurse busied herself checking and recording Marcia's observations. They were all within normal limits. Claudia leant forward and kissed Marcia on her forehead, and said, "I am going to leave you now and go and fetch Marcus. He won't be long."

Chapter Five

C laudia returned to Marcus' room. She knocked on the door and entered. Marcus was asleep. He was lying on the bed just as she had left him. She called to him and when he eventually responded she told him the news. Marcus sat up in bed and rubbed his eyes.

"Is she alright?"

Claudia smiled and nodded her head.

"She is expecting you. I told her I sent you to bed because you had spent all your time with her and that you were exhausted."

"Will you come with me to see her? Please? I am afraid to go alone. I love her so much. I am frightened of losing her."

"Of course, I will come with you. That is why I am here; to support you and Marcia."

It took Marcus some time to get out of bed. He went to the bathroom and when he returned he was ready to accompany Claudia to the intensive care unit. When they arrived, the staff were making arrangements to transfer Marcia to a high dependency unit. Claudia consulted with the staff while Marcus rushed to Marcia's bedside. She was relieved to see him. Marcus was overwhelmed with joy as he embraced his wife. She was sleepy and kept asking why she was in hospital. He clung to her, caressing her and removing the hair from her face. They looked closely at each other prior to Marcus speaking.

"It is good to see you. I am so happy you are back with me. I was worried about you and the baby."

Marcia lifted herself up but she was weakened by her experience and rested her head back on her pillow.

"The baby? Is the baby all right?"

"Yes. The baby is all right. Claudia has been looking after him. He is in the baby unit and the nurses are enchanted with him. They say he is beautiful and contented and I agree with them." Marcus smiled.

"What happened? Why am I in hospital?"

"You developed a fever, fell asleep and I couldn't wake you."

"Am I alright now?"

"Yes. The nurses are taking you to another unit until you are well enough to come home."

* * *

The staff arrived to relocate Marcia. Claudia and Marcus went to see Dr Jameson, as they wanted to leave Marcia to settle into her new routine and be reunited with her baby.

Dr Jameson welcomed the visitors into his office with an outstretched hand. He was pleased that Marcia's recovery was progressing satisfactorily.

"Good afternoon Dr Jameson. Thank you for seeing us and for all the help and support from you and your team," said Marcus.

Dr Jameson nodded and smiled.

"We were lucky that Marcia came to us while she was still responsive. It often helps in these circumstances, though thankfully they are rare. Please, do sit down. You must have several questions to ask me."

Marcus and Claudia sat in the chairs provided. Marcus spoke.

"Thank you Dr Jameson. I don't know where to begin. So much has happened in a short space of time. My life has been transformed so rapidly and I am unsure how I will cope with the changes."

"Don't worry, we will get you and Marcia some professional help. It will make the transition easier for you both and help you to cope with your situation. Please have the assurance that you may contact me if you feel I can help. And, of course, you have the loyalty of your sister."

Marcus looked at Claudia and smiled. Claudia nodded her head in agreement. Dr Jameson continued.

"We need to do some further tests on Marcia. Now she is awake I will have a chat with her to gain her consent. We also need to test her family and complete more tests on you and the baby. It's all part of DNA profiling and it's nothing to worry about."

Marcus squinted his eyes and shifted himself in the chair. He appeared uncomfortable by this statement, as he said, "Doctor, Marcia has no relatives. She is an only child and her parents, who were only children, died a few years ago. Is there a problem? Do I need to have concerns?"

"Some medical tests ask for further information. We may be able to leave Marcus Aurelius alone as it is hospital policy to retain placentas for anonymous research. I am hopeful we can retrieve the information we need from that specimen. As soon as we have a conclusion we will let you know. Have you any further questions?"

Claudia narrowed her eyes and furrowed her brow. She was about to speak but Dr Jameson looked at her and shook his head as if willing her to remain silent.

Marcus stared at the floor for a while prior to his response. He seemed unable to focus his gaze on the doctor because he was fazed by the unfolding events. "Would the tests results be affected by Marcia not having relatives?" Marcus asked.

"No. We will work around that. She has the baby," Dr Jameson responded.

Marcus continued staring at the floor for a long time prior to speaking. Claudia remained silent.

"I have many, many questions but I am unable to formulate them. I cannot cope with anything at present. Please do whatever you know is best for me and my family."

Marcus paused for a while as though unsure how to proceed, then said, "I have to spend some time with Marcia and Marcus Aurelius. Then we will have questions to ask you."

"Thank you Dr Jameson. My brother and I appreciate all that you and your team are doing to help our family at this troubling time. We will return to see Marcia, then Marcus must get some rest."

"I quite agree with you Claudia. Marcus needs to rest. He has had a difficult time. It is good that you are here to help him."

Claudia and Marcus took leave of Dr Jameson. Marcus went to see Marcia, and Claudia returned to Marcus' room. She paced up and down. She was perplexed. In fact, she was completely baffled by what Dr Jameson was not saying. His tone and manner were reassuring, but as a doctor she knew that he was hiding something from Marcus. Why did he request further tests from Marcus and more tests from Marcia and the placenta? Something was wrong. Something was disturbingly wrong. It just did not add up.

She wondered if Marcia had a genetic medical condition and they were testing her to ascertain whether it had been passed on to the baby. She sat in the chair and her mind raced through the knowledge she had accrued from her research. She knew that it would be unethical to request an interview with Dr Jameson on her own but she resolved to speak to her boss in an effort to be reassured.

She thought about her mother. The relationship was icy. Mama was angry with her for supporting Marcia and refused to speak to her when she telephoned. She was deeply upset by this exclusion. Claudia felt unsettled but was unable to discuss her feelings with Marcus. She did not want to add to his anguish. She felt her loyalty was to Marcia, as she had no family to support her.

Claudia went to the hotel to speak with her mother and aunt. It was not to be. They had left. Her family had returned to Andorra and were unaware of the events taking place. At least Dr Jameson had reassured them that Marcia should make a full recovery and would remain in hospital a few more days until it was safe for her to return home. Arrangements were also made for the flat to be checked and cleaned to ensure that there was no risk of reinfection when Marcia and the baby returned.

Chapter Six

It was a difficult journey returning to Andorra for Maria. She was silent for most of the time. Whenever her sister attempted to speak to her she was rebuffed. Maria was in no mood to listen or speak to anyone. She was racked with guilt, shame and anger. Her thoughts were with her late husband. They had been married for thirty-five years, and since his death two years ago she had missed her children, especially Marcus. He was her pride and joy. When he was born she felt complete. It was different when Claudia was born; she really wanted a boy, and was disappointed, but she hid her disappointment from everyone.

She had many happy memories. Family life was successful, unremarkable and as normal as their friends' and other families in the village. It only became difficult when Marcus became ill at the age of thirteen. It unsettled her more than it did her husband. She secretly wished that it were Claudia who should be ill, not Marcus. The doctors explained that he had to be isolated because he had contracted a particularly virulent form of mumps. She became agitated. One of Marcus' friends had developed mumps encephalitis and died as a result, so extra caution was necessary. She was devastated but kept up the pretence of being able to cope. She sent Claudia away as she could not bear to see her being well when Marcus was ill.

She spent every day, and well into the night, at his bedside in the hospital, worrying and thinking that she might lose him. She forsook her husband and daughter. Only Marcus mattered as she shored up unrealistic guilt. When he recovered she continued holding on to that feeling, and spent his teenage years attempting to make up for what she perceived was her fault. A concealed memory from the past overshadowed her, as she fought to gain control of her feelings. In subsequent years she insisted on having his fertility tested yearly, until he decided that enough was enough.

When he was at university, his girlfriends all disappeared and that impacted her guilt further. Eventually he told her that marriage was not for him. She still hoped that there was a girl somewhere that was brave enough to love Marcus. He was handsome, so making friends was easy. The problem was his inability to father children. She reflected again on Claudia's birth, remembering her disappointment that it was a girl, but Claudia had grown into a person she could relate to. When Marcus came along she soon forgot her displeasure.

Now, what she saw as a betrayal was, for her, terrifying. A feeling of all-encompassing guilt consumed her being, as she reflected on her childhood and the events that had shaped her life. She had resigned herself to the fact that grandchildren from Marcus were not possible. She had felt pain at each rejection from his relationships. As a mother, she loved her son and she grieved for him. Now, this. What was a mother to do? When he met Marcia she felt she could relax because Marcus was no longer alone. She disliked the girl but decided to place her faith in Marcia. She saw her as the perfect companion for her son. Marcia was sweet and shy and did not have any family of her own, but the shock of Marcia's perceived infidelity brought back all the traumatic memories of her life and overwhelmed her. Mama felt she could not go through this renewed pain and suffering. When Marcus sided with Marcia and Claudia agreed with him, she felt that the betrayal was complete.

She lay on her bed and wept.

Chapter Seven

D r Jameson sat at the desk in his office. Across from him sat Dr William Ellam. He was the Forensic Pathologist at the Hospital. Dr Ellam had made a personal visit to see Dr Jameson. He was concerned as the Buccal Tests and subsequent DNA blood assays seeking the 24hr markers in the samples from Marcus, Marcia and Marcus Aurelius were conclusive but baffling. Dr Ellam had been called in by the laboratory technician to check the results of the first samples and had requested the subsequent repeats. He wanted additional clarification of the results. As he suspected, the results were irrefutable. Now, here he was, sitting across the room from Dr Jameson and about to reveal the results.

When Dr Jameson received the telephone call from Dr Ellam requesting an urgent meeting he was surprised. But nothing could have prepared him for what was about to be revealed.

"We have a problem with the test results. After the Buccal tests I was called in because it was necessary, due to the expense, that I certify repeat tests to include additional blood assays. The first test is always repeated on the initial sample to minimise a false result. It is unusual, even rare, for further tests except, perhaps, for judicial reviews in paternity cases. The sample you requested was for peace of mind for a mother to be reconciled with her son and daughter in law. However, it opened up a world of untold mystery."

"Is Marcus the baby's father?" Dr Jameson asked.

"Undoubtedly. There is no question that Marcus is the biological father of the baby. The question is," Dr Ellam paused, and looked directly at Dr Jameson, "Who is the mother?"

Dr Jameson took a sharp intake of breath.

"I don't understand. I delivered Marcia myself and Marcus Aurelius is the same baby that I delivered. Sorry Doctor, but I do not follow."

"Let me explain. As you are aware, under normal circumstances, a child inherits half of its DNA from the father and half from the mother. The conclusion of a test is based on the theory that if a man shares certain sequences with a child then the likelihood is that he is the biological father of that child. For maximum probability of paternity, the mother, the child and the alleged father are tested."

"I know genetics is not my field of expertise, but..." Dr Jameson interrupted.

Dr Ellam smiled.

"What is happening here has required extensive research on my part. And there is a lot more that we have to consider before we arrive at a definitive conclusion. We were as baffled as you are now. Perhaps, more so. Allow me to elucidate."

"Sorry to interrupt you, but I am trying to understand. Please, please continue." Dr Jameson said.

Dr Ellam nodded and continued.

"It took me some time to get an understanding, and I still have reservations as there are huge gaps to fill. There needs to be a comparison of the child's sample against both of the adults. In the first instance the cheeks of all the individuals were swabbed. The results were consistent with the hypothesis that the alleged father was indeed the true biological father of the baby. The same tests showed that the adult female, whose sample we tested, was not the biological mother of the baby. She does not have the expected biological profile required to be the baby's mother."

"It's impossible. I delivered Marcia of Marcus Aurelius myself. There must be some mistake."

Dr Ellam frowned.

"That is the reason I was called in to authorise further tests and why I requested an urgent meeting with you. Now, from the days in the 1950s when I was a trainee pathologist, new research with blood typing for transfusions showed discrepancies and changes in blood profiles in some patients, post-transfusions. It became apparent that some people had more than one blood type. At that time they were secretly referred to as "blood chimeras" after the Greek myth – the

Chimera. I have spent the last three days doing research on the topic, and have some startling information. I am close to having an answer, but it raises more questions. My American colleagues have been a great help. They have had two cases and have been advising me on possible outcomes."

Dr Jameson shook his head. He was attempting to digest the information that was being imparted to him. Of course he remembered the impact that blood transfusions had on changing the blood profile of some recipients. He had experienced that as a trainee obstetrician but he was unsure how a woman giving birth was not the biological mother of the baby. He knew that Marcia and Marcus had not received any formal treatment in order to conceive. It was pure chance that he was the duty consultant for the hospital when Marcia arrived with abdominal pain.

He pondered the implications before saying, "Where do we go from here?"

"There is a legal angle to this. Now that paternity is established, we are empowered to ascertain the maternal parentage of the baby. In effect, the burden is now on the alleged mother to prove that the baby belongs to her. How well do you know Marcia?"

"I first saw Marcia about four years ago. It was soon after she was married. At that time she was having gynaecological problems. After surgical intervention everything settled and I did not see her again until she arrived to give birth."

"Do you know whether she has had any other operations? The results may be helpful," Dr Ellam said.

"No. Not that I am aware of but I will check her documents and get back to you," Dr Jameson responded.

Dr Ellam paused for a moment, then he continued.

"The Chimera myth is about a fire-breathing monster with the head of a lion, the body of a goat and the tail of a serpent. As you will no doubt remember, in human biology, a Chimera is an organism with at least two genetically distinct types of cells, or someone meant to be a twin. This can be the result of two fertilised eggs, fusing to become one foetus *in utero* that carries two distinct genetic codes – two different strands of DNA. It is an exceptionally rare condition with only thirty cases, to date, ever reported worldwide. In such cases we reckon that each strand has a different DNA makeup. Therefore, if we test samples from different parts of the body we will, hopefully, obtain DNA matches for them. But not necessarily. We have carried out extensive tests on the placenta, but to no avail. We also understand that Marcia has no living relatives. Our only hope now is to obtain some internal tissue samples to test for traces of a genetic link."

"What sort of samples are we looking at here? I am finding your research fascinating and I will help in any way I can," Dr Jameson said.

"Well, I know from my research that lymphatic tissue and tissue from the organs of the endocrine system are most likely to reveal a match, but, there is a degree of risk and uncertainty. Our hypothesis is that Marcia has given birth to her twin's baby. This can occur when one twin dies in the early stages of pregnancy, and because of a shared placenta the surviving twin, as an adult, unwittingly carries the dead twin's DNA. This can be transmitted via deposits of stem cells in the bone marrow of the surviving twin. Hence, the surviving twin retains her own DNA but any offspring potentially can only receive the deceased twin's DNA. In the absence of a family member we are unable to establish legally the baby's maternal parent from the DNA samples."

"You keep using the word 'legally'. I suspect that you have a reason?" Dr Jameson said.

"Yes, I do," Dr Ellam responded. "It is in Marcia's interests to register with the courts that she is the maternal parent of the baby. She will require proof and that is usually DNA. There are enormous legal challenges and previously unseen hazards as a result of the test."

"For instance?" Dr Jameson appeared perplexed.

"She could be accused of stealing someone else's baby, or not being able to give consent if the baby became ill. At worst, if Marcus were to be incapacitated the baby could be removed from her care and placed in the guardianship of his family, or even adopted as there is no genetic link to prove that she is the mother."

Dr Jameson remained silent for an inordinate amount of time as he mulled over the information. When he finally spoke his voice was muted.

"When I offered the family DNA testing I had no idea of the implications or even expected a scenario such as this. I have never had a result open to unusual interpretation. I need some time to assimilate this so we can disseminate what we have learnt. I have to say that Marcus' sister, Claudia, is a postdoctoral research associate in genetics, so it will make our task much easier when we interview the family. I believe she already suspects that something is wrong, but she has kept quiet."

Dr Ellam stood up. He handed Dr Jameson a file and said, "This will help. It contains all the information I have gathered so far. You will find it helpful but we must meet again soon to discuss the best way forward. Thank you, Dr Jameson. I look forward to hearing from you soon."

Dr Jameson stood up and extended his hand and said, "Thank you for the insightful information you have shared with me. I will read the file as a priority and get back to you as soon as possible. It is a pleasure to meet you. I look forward to our next meeting with great interest."

Dr Ellam shook his hand as they made their way to the door. After his departure Dr Jameson sat at his desk and buried his head in his hands. When he finally raised his head, he opened the file, and began to read.

Chapter Eight

The following morning, Dr Jameson wandered into the room where Marcus and Claudia were sitting. He had requested to see them in the relatives' room as opposed to the formality of his office. He wanted to put them at ease in a relaxed environment so he could discuss Dr Ellam's findings. The DNA results had been a shock for him. It had created an entirely new problem that he felt sure would cause the family unavoidable anxiety. He wondered about Marcus, as he knew that he was struggling to cope emotionally.

He had thought long and hard about the approach he would take, and finally decided to see Marcus and Claudia prior to involving Marcia. He would take his cue from them and give them the option of briefing Marcia before the formal interview to include Dr Ellam. He was especially grateful to have Claudia present, because he felt her presence would aid Marcus' understanding, as well as support him. He had taken the opportunity to apprise Claudia's boss, Dr Kate Smith, of Dr Ellam's findings. It was opportune to have a confidential discussion with her as Claudia had asked for his help to secure compassionate leave. Claudia was reluctant to leave her brother. She always felt responsible for him.

The pair greeted him warmly. Marcus smiled as he stood up to shake Dr Jameson's outstretched hand and said, "Good morning, Dr Jameson. We saw Marcia briefly and she is making rapid progress. The staff are pleased with her."

"Yes, I too saw her briefly. She is doing much better than we expected. In medicine we would refer to her progress as a statistical outliner rather than a miracle, but secretly we feel it's a miracle," Dr Jameson said, feeling pleased with himself and smiling.

Claudia laughed as she greeted him and they sat down.

"Claudia, I have spoken to your boss and she has given you compassionate leave. She was pleased to hear of your devotion to your family at this sensitive time."

"Thank you Dr Jameson. I am indebted to you. I just could not leave Marcus, Marcia and the baby. It would break my heart. Thank you for your intervention."

"It is my pleasure. I am delighted to be able to help," Dr Jameson responded.

Dr Jameson paused. He always found it best, when dealing with relatives, to speak as little as possible to allow them time to absorb what was being said. Claudia smiled and looked intently at the doctor.

Dr Jameson continued.

"I wanted to see you both. I stress that this is an informal chat and it would not be taking place but for Claudia's specific knowledge."

Marcus stared at the doctor, then began to fidget prior to speaking.

"Doctor, do I need to be alarmed? Are Marcia and the baby all right? I am a little concerned. When you asked to see us I must admit I began to worry again. Marcia is my whole world and now I have a son I need her more than ever."

Dr Jameson looked directly at Marcus and said, "Marcus, please try not to worry. Your wife has made a remarkable recovery and the baby is also doing well. Yes, they both are perfectly fine but we are having certain challenges with the blood results, but it is nothing to be concerned about that will affect your family medically."

Marcus shuddered as Dr Jameson continued speaking.

"The hospital pathologist, Dr Ellam, and I will see you with Marcia to discuss the blood results. However, I felt I ought to have a private chat with you first to prepare you for what was to come."

Marcus wrung his hands in agitation but Claudia spoke up.

"I knew something was not quite right. Has Marcia got a blood disorder?"

"Yes and no," responded Dr Jameson. "Neither Marcia or the baby have any blood disorders but the tests have revealed some interesting unexpected results."

He turned and spoke directly to Marcus.

"Marcus, there is no need for you to be afraid. Marcus Aurelius and you are well and, I repeat, we expect that Marcia will make a full recovery. That is not the challenge we are experiencing."

Dr Jameson leaned forward and looked first at Claudia, and then narrowed his eyes as he spoke to Marcus.

"You see, we are faced with a rare occurrence that does not directly affect the medical wellbeing of any of the parties. Marcus, you already know that you are the biological father of Marcus Aurelius, but Marcia, according to the DNA sample, is not the biological mother."

Both Marcus and Claudia gasped.

"That can't be right. I don't believe you," Marcus said, with a hint of sarcasm in his voice. "You told me that you delivered Marcia, so how is it possible that she is not the biological mother of our baby? That's impossible."

Claudia remained silent but looked intently at Dr Jameson as he continued to focus on Marcus.

"I was sceptical myself when the pathologist told me the results of the blood test. Remember, I told you that I delivered your wife so I know that she gave birth to Marcus Aurelius. Sometimes in medicine we don't always have all the answers. I will do my best to explain this unusual occurrence. Please hear..."

Marcus interrupted.

"You are not making sense. You keep repeating that you delivered Marcia with our baby yet you are now saying that she is not Marcus Aurelius' mother. Why are you saying those things?"

Dr Jameson pursed his lips then looked at Claudia.

"Claudia, I need to speak to you directly about the tests results. You are at the beginning of your research into comparative genetics. The condition that Marcia has presented with is extremely rare. Although she gave birth to Marcus Aurelius it would appear that there is no DNA match between her and the baby. Dr Ellam, the hospital pathologist, discussed the details with me. It is outside of my sphere of expertise but I am learning the rudiments of this very special case and I feel certain that you will find it of interest in your research. For now, your continued support will be invaluable to your brother and his wife."

Claudia eyes widened and she looked upwards and sighed. She was disturbed by the concept but was uncertain how to react. She looked uncomprehendingly at the doctor. Her face showed struggle and distress, and her inability to comprehend was apparent. Finally she spoke in a controlled voice.

"Doctor, I have to admit that I am confused. I need more information in order to understand what seems to me to be quite complex."

"As you know, I delivered Marcia myself so in my mind there is no question about Marcus Aurelius' maternal parentage. However, Dr Ellam suggests that Marcia is one of a set of twins, her sibling having died *in utero* in early pregnancy. This episode would have been unknown to Marcia's mother. What possibly transpired was that the blood supply of her twin continued to support Marcia's survival while only registering the imprint of her deceased twin. As a result, Marcia appears to have given birth to her sister's baby."

Claudia raised her eyebrows and the look of horror deepened on her face. Marcus bent forward and gave a laboured, mournful cry. After much hesitation, Claudia said, "Are we to understand that Marcus Aurelius only belongs to Marcus, and that he has no mother? Or at worst, his mother never lived but has given birth to Marcus Aurelius through Marcia? I am not sure how that is possible."

Dr Jameson responded in a subdued tone.

"Put another way, Marcus Aurelius' biological mother is his deceased aunt. Matters are complicated because Marcia has no living relatives from whom we can obtain DNA samples. It now becomes a legal discussion to enshrine her in law as the mother of Marcus Aurelius."

Marcus listened intently as the doctor spoke directly to Claudia. Then he said, "Dr Jameson, you told me that Marcia and I are the baby's parents. This mention of the law and the implication that Marcia is not our baby's mother is impossible for me to understand. When Marcia is well enough can we please take our baby home?"

"It's not that simple. I understand your inability to comprehend what I am saying, but I wanted to see you both personally and give you the opportunity to assimilate this unusual information. I thought it would make it easier for you both to support Marcia when Dr Ellam and I interview you. He is well-equipped to answer all your queries and help you to provide solutions."

Marcus interrupted the doctor.

"Doctor, I don't believe what I am hearing. I cannot understand what you are saying about my wife and baby." He shook his head from side to side and continued. "I can't take any more of this. What is Marcia going to say? Before, I was not the father. Now, she is not the mother. It's too much… too much. Do you hear? It is too much for me to cope with. I can't take any more. I just want to take my wife and baby home."

Marcus rocked backwards and forwards clasping his arms around his chest. Claudia got up and went over to Marcus and held his hand. Dr Jameson looked at Claudia, who had remained silent at Marcus' outburst, and then spoke directly to Marcus.

"Marcus, I chose to exclude Marcia from this conversation. I wanted you to be aware first and give you time to ask questions. You can then prepare Marcia, so eventually we can divulge the details and cause her minimal distress. I am very much aware that it was stress that brought her to the hospital in the first instance, and as her doctor, I have a duty of care towards her. This is partly the reason that I am seeing you without Marcia being present. I need you and your sister to have an understanding of the implications of the blood test. I have to be certain that you understand that Marcia is the priority here and that we must ensure that mentally she is supported during this unusual event."

There was an eerie silence in the room prior to Marcus speaking.

"Dr Jameson, my wife and I are very close. I knew instinctively that Marcus Aurelius was my baby. A dream that I never thought possible. Every day Marcia continues to improve. I do not understand the complexity of what is happening. I expect Claudia will have a better understanding. But as for me, I just want to take my wife and baby home."

Dr Jameson spoke reassuringly to Marcus.

"Don't worry, Marcus. All is not as daunting as it seems. At least you will be able to reassure your mother that you are indeed the baby's father and bring the extended family back together again."

Marcus buried his head in his hands. Claudia put her arms around him and responded.

"Doctor, Mama will not speak to us. This is primarily the reason for Marcus' distress. So, after Dr Ellam sees us, I will call my aunt and give her the news. It will be better if she speaks to our mother. My aunt stays with our mother so it may not be possible to speak with her. Also, if we say too much now, Mama may want to visit and that will cause complications."

Dr Jameson paused for a moment, then nodded and said, "That seems to be the best way forward. I will arrange with Dr Ellam a convenient time to meet and get back to you. I will leave now but if either of you have any questions, you know you can call me anytime."

Marcus gave Dr Jameson a look of resignation, but before he could speak, Dr Jameson said to him, "Perhaps you need some time together with Claudia. I could see you both again, if it helps, prior to Dr Ellam's meeting with the family."

Claudia spoke.

"Dr Jameson, we are grateful to you. Marcus and I will discuss what we have heard and wait to hear from you. Thank you for taking the time to share this information without Marcia being present. I agree it would have been too stressful for her to witness our reaction to this complex news. It certainly is alarming, having given birth to a baby, a baby that you were not expecting, then to be told that you are not the biological mother. Marcus and I will brief Marcia and ensure that she does not experience any unnecessary stress that would inhibit her recovery."

Dr Jameson gave a half smile and said, "Thank you Claudia." He then turned to Marcus and said, "I will do all that I can to help in the resolution of this challenge that we are facing. Meanwhile it is good that you have the support of your sister."

After Dr Jameson took his leave Marcus and Claudia sat down in silence, which was broken when Marcus erupted in tears.

Chapter Nine

Dr Jameson returned to his office and arranged a meeting with Dr Ellam to see the family the following day. He telephoned Marcus and apprised him of the situation. Marcus appeared more in control and seemed eager for the process to begin.

Dr Jameson then stared out of the oriel window at the little copse of trees, observing the sunlight as it glistened on the leaves. The blizzard of information he received from Dr Ellam unnerved him. It caused him to reflect on his life as a doctor, and the implications of all the actions he had taken when dealing with patients and their relatives. He was on difficult terrain in this particular case. He knew that navigation would probably create more problems than it solved, but he was determined to offer hope to the family to which he had become attached. Dr Ellam had briefed him on the legal aspect of the case, and he felt responsible for requesting the DNA test. The results had been a shock. In truth, his actions had the opposite effect of what was intended. He felt culpable, and it was this feeling that propelled him to leave his office and go to see Marcia.

He arrived to find that she and Marcus Aurelius had been moved to a non-specialist unit, but he had not been informed. He was told that Marcia no longer required specific medical and nursing care, hence the transfer. This situation normally left him frustrated but today he was unperturbed. When he arrived on the new unit, he found Marcus and Claudia in animated conversation with Marcia. The baby was asleep in his cot.

"Hello, everyone. I just came to see that Marcia has settled into her new environment," he said to everyone as he observed Marcia.

Marcia laughed and said, "Good afternoon, Dr Jameson. This room is comfortable, with a view of the lawn and flowerbed. I can even see the garden when I am in bed, and the nurses have been very kind. I feel spoilt."

Dr Jameson smiled and Marcia continued.

"I understand from Marcus that we are to be seen by you and another doctor tomorrow. I am curious about this development with my blood results. I am just happy to be alive and have a beautiful baby boy and a family who cares for me."

Dr Jameson walked over to the bed and said, "It's good to see you, Marcia. I expect Marcus told you that you will be staying with us for a bit longer."

"Yes, he did," Marcia responded. "Claudia has been explaining some aspects of the medical dilemma. But as long as the baby is alright, I am happy."

Dr Jameson smiled and said, "That is good to hear. I don't want you getting stressed about anything else. I just came to see that you had settled in."

"Yes, all the staff have been kind and helpful. In fact, everyone has been amazing," said Marcia.

"Good. Good. We always pride ourselves on the quality of care we provide for patients and their families. If there is anything you need, please don't hesitate to ask. Meanwhile, I will see you tomorrow," Dr Jameson told Marcia. He then turned to Marcus and Claudia and said, "Thank you for all that you do to help Marcia. I will see you all tomorrow evening with Dr Ellam."

* * *

It was early evening the next day when Dr Jameson and Dr Ellam entered Marcia's room. She was resting, cradling the baby in her arms with a look of contentment on her face. Marcus and Claudia stood up and Dr Jameson introduced Dr Ellam to the family.

They exchanged pleasantries and chatted until there was a knock on the door and a nursing sister entered. She introduced herself and then sat down next to Marcia's bedside.

Dr Ellam began the discussion.

"I understand that my colleague has already briefed you with some aspects of the blood samples we received for DNA testing. I will use medical terminology that may possibly be unfamiliar but you are free to express any feelings or ask any questions to me or Dr Jameson."

Dr Ellam looked around the room prior to continuing.

"We examined all the data, and the term '*not excluded*' was applied to Marcus' DNA sample. This suggests that he is the biological father of Marcus Aurelius. To our surprise, when we compared Marcia's sample with the DNA of the baby, the results were '*excluded*', which means Marcia is not the biological mother of Marcus Aurelius. We were intrigued by the result, so we repeated it a few times to ascertain its credibility."

True to form, Marcia looked at Marcus and said, "Mama will be so happy when she hears this news. She will have a grandson that she never expected to have."

Everyone in the room except Claudia was surprised by her response. Marcus visibly relaxed. Dr Jameson was especially pleased and asked if anyone had any questions. With none forthcoming, Dr Ellam continued. He appeared to relish the knowledge that he had accrued. He told the family that there would be legal implications that would apply to a birth mother whose DNA was not replicated by her offspring. He requested that Marcia remain in hospital until the hospital legal team could finalise all arrangements for her to be recognised as the legal mother of Marcus Aurelius. The family listened intently to the facts he provided with some degree of surprise and resignation. Marcus, made confident by his wife and sister's acceptance, was amenable to the suggestions.

With the discussion ended, the doctors withdrew. The nursing sister remained for a while. She reassured Marcia that she and the baby would be hospitalised until the process of legalising her as Marcus Aurelius' mother was established. She explained that this was to ensure the hospital's legal team could handle the case. If Marcia were discharged she would be responsible for initiating procedures to prove parentage of Marcus Aurelius. Also, there was a degree of uncertainty as to whether the hospital could legally discharge the baby into Marcia's care. At present, the hospital legal team were unable to obtain any known precedents that had been established for a case as rare as this one. It was therefore suggested that it would be prudent, due to the potential of the cost incurred being astronomical, that Marcia remained in the care of the hospital. If the family decided that Marcia was to return home they would have to instruct a legal team. Representation by the hospital would then be untenable, as the hospital would be obliged to represent itself to avoid a conflict of interest. As it stood, the hospital's legal team was already acquiring documented evidence from the staff that were present when Marcia arrived at the hospital. Handing over any information to another legal team would incur cost and cause unnecessary delays. Holding on to this case would also allow the hospital to acquire knowledge for use in any subsequent cases of a similar nature. With the advent of IVF and tri-parent siblings, the research gained from this case could be vital to the hospital in future. The hospital was willing to be responsible for all the charges incurred as a result of the forthcoming legal proceedings.

Everyone agreed that this was best. The nursing sister left the room and the conversation revolved around Mama and finding the best way to communicate with her. Marcia lay in bed, observing her sleeping baby. She had listened intently to the intricate nature of the discussion but her thoughts were with motherhood and her new role of caring for her baby.

She called to Marcus and murmured, "He looks just like you with his mop of black curls. I am so happy for Mama. She loves you so much and was always unhappy that you could not be a father. Now, when she hears this news, she will not be unhappy and blame herself anymore."

Marcus looked at his wife with renewed feelings of love and smiled.

"In spite of all the awful things Mama said about you and the baby you still find it in your heart to think of her happiness. I love you Marcia. I love you with all of my heart. I feel blessed having you in my life."

Marcia looked at Marcus and her face filled with joy.

"I love you Marcus. You must not be too hard on Mama as she only ever thinks of your happiness. She must have been overwhelmed by the shock of the birth to say the things that she said. When she hears this news about the DNA results, that you are a father, that you have a son, all her anxieties will melt away and she will be the same loving mother to you and Claudia."

Marcus and Claudia walked over to Marcia's bedside and embraced her. They were both overwhelmed by her words. Their eyes were moist with tears.

"Thank you Marcia. You are the sister I always wanted and I love you," Claudia whispered.

Marcus looked at his wife as he wiped his tearstained face and repeated, "I love you Marcia. Thank you for making me a father and giving me a son. You are right. Mama will be happy for us to be a family again when she hears the news."

Chapter Ten

Maria awoke in the morning to the sunrays streaming through her bedroom window, highlighting the subtle shade of pink wallpaper that covered the walls. The focal point in the room was a dark pink padded headboard that created a sense of opulence. The deep-pile cream carpet on the floor gave an essence of warmth and comfort to the space. There was an array of brightly coloured cushions on the ottoman at the foot of the bed, with a folded multi-coloured blanket that added a sense of style. The bed linen was white, interspersed with pink and brown hues, which were an excellent match for the luxurious drapes that adorned the windows. A chaise longue graced the right side of the room. Subdued lighting completed the ambience that Maria so adored.

Her eyes were red and swollen and her body ached. She wept long into the night as she rehearsed over and over again the events that had occurred in Marcus' flat. Her feelings were compounded by the isolation she felt at what she perceived was the loss of not only Marcus but her daughter as well. How could they desert her like that? Did they not remember that Marcus was unable to have children?

Maria squinted as the sunlight caught her eyes and they hurt. She held her head in her hands in an effort to control the throbbing pain. She forced herself out of bed and hobbled to the bathroom. It was tiled in a black and white hexagonal pattern. In the far corner was a white porcelain bath with twin matching pedestal basins and saniware. Two Abbey chairs were situated on either side. To the left on the wall was a large mirrored cabinet. She fumbled in the cabinet hoping to find a tablet to soothe her aching head. The contents of the cupboard fell at her feet creating a resounding sound. She winced as she knelt on the tiled floor and retrieved a blister strip of pain relief tablets. She stood up, extracted two, swallowed them with the aid of a glass of water, then returned to her bed.

She pondered her relationship with Marcia. Maria was cordial and gave the impression that she had accepted Marcia into the family. Secretly, she disliked the girl. She felt her son deserved better. It didn't help that they were besotted with each other. This evoked jealousy in her. Marcia was a nice enough girl, but she was now the object of Marcus' affection and this, Maria felt, side-lined her. She watched as Marcus relied more and more on Marcia, and that shift away from her filled her with a great sense of loss. It simply enhanced her antipathy towards the girl. All her submerged feelings of hatred directed at Marcia came to the fore. Claudia embraced Marcia as a sister with such intensity that it further contributed to Maria's discomfort. Outwardly she appeared calm and in control, but inwardly she harboured a hatred towards her daughter-in-law which she thought no one suspected.

When Marcus telephoned about the baby, she was enraged. She called her sister and discussed what she saw as an impossible situation. On arrival at the flat in London, when she saw the three of them together and Claudia's loyalty towards them, she was no longer able to control her rage. She erupted. The venom with which she greeted Marcia frightened her and left her feeling ashamed. She felt that as a result of her behaviour towards her daughter-in-law she had lost her children, and her heart was in pain. Now, lying in bed, unable to rationalise her feelings of insecurity and shame, she wept.

Magdalena was worried about her sister. Maria had spent the last two days in bed, refusing to communicate except to acknowledge the refreshments her sister brought her. She forbade Magdalena from answering the telephone. Every time it rang, Magdalena paced up and down the drawing room waiting for it to stop. It was an ornate room lined with light oak panels. The walls above were decorated in the palest of cream. A pair of two-seater oak-framed sofas and two matching single armchairs in a deeper cream, with scatter cushions of various pastel colours, adorned the room. The occasional table housed three or four fireside books, but, in pride of place, stood a black baby grand piano in the left corner of the room. A family portrait and a blue-and-white porcelain vase of autumn orchids were displayed on it.

At lunchtime, Magdalena was sitting in the drawing room next to the telephone when it rang. Instinctively she answered it. Claudia was on the line.

"How are you, Auntie Magdalena? How is Mama? I have been calling but without success. Is something wrong with the phone? It just keeps ringing."

"No. There is nothing wrong with the phone. Your mother is very angry and upset. She has taken to her bed. She refuses to speak and has forbidden me from answering the phone. She will not discuss either you or Marcus. She feels you both have betrayed her," Magdalena said in an angry voice.

"Auntie, I am so sorry, but I have wonderful news for Mama," Claudia said with a ring of excitement in her voice, ignoring the anger in her aunt's voice.

"Well, I hope you can cheer her up and get her to smile again. I can't begin to tell you how unhappy she is. I am so worried. The twins have been deeply upset and I am at my wits' end," Magdalena responded.

"Please Auntie. I will not upset Mama. I must speak to her. There have been important developments and I have some exciting news to tell her. Please Auntie. I must talk to Mama," Claudia said.

"I will do my best but please don't upset your mother anymore. There is already a terrible atmosphere in the house and the twins and I are finding it very difficult to cope. Hold on," Magdalena said in a conciliatory tone.

After a short time Maria answered the call. She was curt.

"What is this news, Claudia? I never thought that my own children, my flesh and blood, would be so disrespectful to me and in front of a *stranger*. I am glad Papa was not there to witness it."

"Mama, I am sorry that we hurt you. We did not intend to cause you pain. Marcus is distressed as Marcia became quite ill after you left. She is in hospital with a high fever but is recovering..."

Mama interrupted Claudia.

"So now you are blaming me again. Is this why you called me? To blame me? I don't want to speak to you," Mama began to shout.

"No, Mama. No. Marcia is recovering and the doctors are hopeful that she will make a complete recovery, but it's a blessing that she became ill. You see, Mama, they carried out a DNA test while she was unconscious and it is proven that Marcus is the baby's father. Mama, you are a grandmother and I am an aunt. I am so happy."

Mama was speechless. The tears stung as they flowed down her cheeks; without responding Mama dropped the phone and ran into her bedroom.

Magdalena hurriedly retrieved the dangling phone and said, "What is it? What did you say to Mama?

Why is she crying? Have you upset her again? I told you not to upset your mother. Life here is extremely difficult without you upsetting your mother even more."

"No. No. No Auntie Magdalena. The news is good. Mama has tears of happiness."

"What is this news that is good that upset your mother further?" Magdalena said sarcastically.

Claudia related the news to her aunt and Magdalena too was filled with tears of joy. She told Claudia that as soon as she could make arrangements they would return to London so Mama could greet her grandchild who was now ten days old.

* * *

Back in her room, Maria locked the door and threw herself onto her bed. She wept uncontrollably and her body convulsed as she buried her head in her pillow in an effort to supress her cries. She banged her fists on the bed. She sat up in bed and struck her chest as she desperately attempted to control her emotions. Maria shook her head as a tragic teenage memory confronted her, leaving her racked with guilt, fear and shame. Maria suddenly had the realisation that the hatred she harboured for Marcia was embedded in her own past, and that past now enveloped her and the fear clawed at her heart. She tossed and turned in the bed crying uncontrollably as she struggled to obliterate her past.

Chapter Eleven

Marcia lay on her bed staring out of the window. She felt better since her discharge from the high dependency unit. She had no recollection about her admission to hospital, and although Marcus and Claudia were supportive she missed her parents. An overwhelming feeling of loneliness enveloped her as she struggled to understand the events of the past few days. Never had she imagined that she would become a mother. It was an unbelievable shock. She was just getting used to the birth when she awoke to find herself again in hospital, surrounded by staff that appeared concerned about her welfare. The baby was a dream. She was indeed the mother of Marcus Aurelius but it seemed unreal.

She recalled seeing Marcus for the first time. She had accidently dropped her gloves in the car park on her way to work. He picked them up and when he handed them to her, their eyes met. There was something about him that aroused her interest. She recalled he was impeccable attired in a dark suit. A dark-grey Crombie overcoat was draped over his shoulders. He held a briefcase in his right hand as he offered her the gloves. She remembered every detail of that first encounter. Her father had a similar overcoat. As a child she had a fascination for the velvet collar. Whenever her father was wearing the coat and he held her in his arms she loved the feel as it brushed against her cheeks. Yes, she missed her parents' closeness. She missed the feelings of joy that would have been experienced had they been alive. She felt grave disappointment that they could not welcome Marcus Aurelius. She fought to hold back the tears, as she did not want anyone to know her sadness.

As an only child she found it difficult to make friends with her peers at the convent school she attended. She was taught by nuns and was attracted to the ethos of becoming one. Marcia had an imaginary friend named Lucy. She relied on her for companionship. They would spend hours playing together in her room. As a child she always felt incomplete and longed for friends. She also desperately wanted a sister, and Lucy filled that void. One day in conversation with her favourite nun, Sister Alyusia, Marcia confided in her about Lucy. The nun told Marcia that it was unhealthy to devote so much time to someone who was not present in life, so, Marcia never mentioned Lucy to anyone again. Lucy remained her special friend and confidant.

Marcia's parents were devout Catholics but advised Marcia to see some of the world prior to formalising her decision to become a Sister of Mercy.

Design Technology at university gave her a different avenue for exploration. In her final year, she was head-hunted by a prestigious company in the city. On completing her studies, she was offered a trainee junior management post. Her aptitude for the job saw her promoted to senior management two years later.

It was a traumatic time for her and she struggled to make decisions about her future. Both her parents had died and she had no relatives to consult. Being unable to make a rational decision about her personal life, she decided to accept the promotion and adopt a 'wait and see' attitude. She enjoyed the work but felt her calling was the Church. She spent long hours praying for guidance. She longed for the companionship that she saw in the Sisters of Mercy but she was hesitant about the commitment that was essential.

As Marcia sat in bed reflecting on her life, she pondered the miracle of the baby's birth. Marcus was her first boyfriend. Prior to meeting him she did not have any interest in boys. Her mind was focused on her work and her Church. Her family were well thought of in their community, and when her parents died she continued her fellowship at the church. She taught at Sunday school and busied herself with activities involving the children. She had an abundance of energy and the children adored her.

Meeting Marcus was a pivotal moment in her life. That morning she was going to arrange a meeting with her boss about leaving the firm to join the Convent. She was nervous as she alighted from the car and dropped her gloves. Her first glimpse of Marcus unsettled her. She did not make that appointment, as she kept thinking about the encounter in the car park. Marcia smiled at the memory as she reflected on her life.

Her parents' birthplace was the historic city of Toledo in Spain, famous for its historic coexistence of Christian, Jewish and Muslim cultures. As a child, her parents often took her to visit the tomb of St Beatriz da Silva y de Menezes and the Monastery of the Immaculate Conception. She recalled conversing with the Franciscan monks on their feast days. Marcia remembered moving from Spain to the outskirts of London where the family settled into the community. It was a different life to the one she was used to in Spain, but the locals embraced the family and the church was welcoming. However, she still missed her time living in Spain and the freedom she had when they lived there. She often had dreams of returning, but she never mentioned them to her parents as they seemed to love their new environment and she did not want to cause them any distress.

Meeting Marcus' parents for the first time was a difficult experience for her. She felt uncomfortable in their presence. They were from the Principality of Andorra. His mother did not appear to welcome her but his father seemed to encourage their relationship. He felt that Marcia would take care of his son. As a father, he had submerged his emotions when he learnt that Marcus was sterile, but when Papa met Marcia for the first time, he immediately recognised in her qualities that evidenced her devotion to his son and the adoration that Marcus had for her. He felt peace and instinctively knew that their marriage was going to work. He knew that he no longer needed to worry about Marcus living a life in solitude.

Mama, on the other hand, had to be persuaded to accept Marcia into her family. Marcia always felt as if she was intruding on her mother-in-law's territory. Maria was pleasant but distant, so Marcia clung to Marcus whenever they were with his parents. Until the baby's birth there was no validation for Marcia's feelings, but the venom with which Mama addressed her that day caused her intense pain. Marcia shivered as memory came flooding back and tears fell from her eyes.

Claudia was different. When they first met, she enveloped Marcia in her arms, saying, "You are just the way Marcus described you."

Claudia turned out to be the friend that Marcia always longed for, and Claudia had found the sister that she always wanted. They bonded from that first meeting and became close, confiding in each other their hopes and dreams. They were just delighted in each other's company. Marcus was especially happy that his sister loved his fiancée, and, even though his mother seemed distant, his parents approved of his relationship.

Chapter Twelve

arcus was troubled. He sat in his room at the hospital. Scattered, broken thoughts flooded his mind. He rehearsed his uneventful journey to New York and the telephone call from Dr Jameson that left him bewildered. He recalled his inability to process what the doctor was telling him. He was tired and thinking of the presentation he was due to give.

He was fortunate as the hotel made all the arrangements for his return flight to London. He thought of Marcia. When he left her at the airport she was well. He wondered if she had an accident. Dr Jameson's tone, as well as his words, did not suggest a negative or life-threatening outcome but he quietly suggested that Marcus should return. Marcus was annoyed that he did not request more information from the doctor. He was so shocked by the unexpected phone call that questions seemed irrelevant at the time. Marcia occupied his thoughts and all he wanted to do was to get back to London as quickly as possible as the doctor had asked.

On the return flight to London, Marcus remembered drifting in and out of sleep. His mind raced ahead of him as he envisioned all manner of catastrophes that may have befallen Marcia. During one disturbing dream he was awoken by the captain's dulcet tone announcing preparations for landing. Marcus was first to alight the aircraft and was fast-tracked through the airport checks to a waiting car that took him directly to the hospital. He caught sight of himself in the rear-view mirror. He was unshaven and looked dishevelled. He ran his fingers through his hair. He barely noticed his surroundings. His mind was preoccupied with Marcia. What was wrong with her? It must be serious otherwise she would have called him. His mind raced ahead of him. Please God, let her be all right. At once he was overwhelmed by a tremendous sense of loss.

"Please God," he said out loud, "don't let her die."

The cab driver looked at him through the mirror and said, "It's only five more minutes to the hospital, sir. They are a good lot there. I am sure that they have been looking after your family. Try not to worry. We're nearly there."

Marcus raised his eyes and looked at him.

"Sorry. It's my wife. I don't know what is wrong with her. The doctor did not tell me. I was just thinking aloud."

The cab driver gave a reassuring smile. Soon the cab came to a halt outside the hospital entrance. The driver got out and helped Marcus retrieve his bag and briefcase.

"Don't worry about the fare, sir. I hope your wife is alright."

He returned to the cab before Marcus could respond. He leaned out of the window and shouted, "Good Luck," as he drove away.

Marcus stood for a brief moment as he collected his thoughts. The taxi driver had been encouraging and Marcus relaxed. He entered the door and made his way towards reception. He introduced himself to the receptionist.

"Good morning. I am Marcus Dos Santos. I believe that Dr Jameson is expecting me."

"Good morning sir. Dr Jameson is expecting you and will be with you shortly," responded the receptionist.

Within minutes, Dr Jameson appeared and introduced himself. Marcus smiled as he remembered the feelings of shock, horror and disbelief as he assimilated Dr Jameson's words.

"Congratulations. Your wife has a beautiful baby boy."

He had imagined many scenarios but none like the one the doctor unveiled. His tears of relief, sadness and elation were overwhelming. He had a son, a baby he never knew he would father. He had missed the birth but when he saw his child for the first time, the surge of love he felt for his wife and son was indescribable. It was surreal.

When Marcia developed puerperal fever his only thought was of her, and his inability to master his feelings was a great source of anxiety for him. He was so bereft that he never thought of ringing his sister for support. All he could focus on was Marcia's illness and that there was a possibility that she might die. Now, as he pondered his lack of ability to cope in a crisis, he thought of how gratifying it was to have Claudia around as she made all the decisions for him. He smiled when he remembered growing up, how she always took care of him. Now his reliance on her was profound.

In the intensive care unit, his reluctance to leave Marcia was driven by fear. As he held her hand, he prayed constantly that God would spare her life. When the doctors and nurses attempted to speak with him, he referred them to Claudia because he knew he was unable to cope with negative news. Claudia proved to be his strength and he relied on her for support. She was also his link between Marcus Aurelius and the nurses who were caring for him.

Remembering brought a wave of emotion of love tinged with sadness. He felt proud to be a father, but feelings of unresolved guilt muddled his thoughts. His mother's hostility towards Marcia caused him to reflect on the way she had reacted with Marcia in the past. He never really took much notice of how his wife was being excluded by his mother. He knew from comments that his mother made that she was jealous of Marcia but he never suspected that she would be vocal in her hatred and cause so much distress and upheaval in the family. His mother's egregious abuse, directed at Marcia, affected him gravely but he was unable to voice it. He always knew that a special bond existed between him and his mother. He loved his mother and he loved his wife and he never wanted to be in a position to have to choose between them. His mother's unprecedented behaviour was forcing him into a position he did not relish. As a result, he felt helpless.

Emotionally, he was disturbed and this caused him to react in an uncharacteristic manner. He was aware that he was developing an inability to manage his emotions but was unsure of a resolution. He felt anger towards Mama that frightened him. She had undoubtedly caused Marcia to become ill. He could not comprehend his mother's behaviour. Yet, in spite of his mother's abuse towards her, Marcia never complained or showed any animosity towards her. She always spoke well of her mother-in-law but seemed to gravitate towards auntie Magdalena.

The duality of anger and love caused Marcus to erupt in tears because he felt powerless and afraid of being forced to make a choice.

He recalled when he himself had mumps; his father would spend long hours in the hospital talking to him. Marcus enjoyed listening to Papa as he spoke about his own life as a young man. Papa had explored

various countries. He learnt their history. He told
Marcus it was a great advantage being able to converse
with local inhabitants in their language. He said it was
fortunate that the people of Andorra were known for
their fluency in at least three languages.

This was the motivation for Marcus reading
History and Languages at university, and taking the
Chair as one of the youngest professors at a highly
prestigious college within the University of London.
Marcus felt a feeling of pride as he thought about his
father. He remembered waking up in that hospital,
seeing the white protective clothing that was worn by
his family, and being frightened. When he heard
Papa's voice through the haze of white he relaxed. His
relationship with his father remained close until his
death. As Marcus sat in his room at this hospital he
wished that Papa was there to hold his hand. Papa
always knew what to do. Now he had a son, Marcia
had recovered and Claudia was supporting him. He
felt safe but troubled.

Chapter Thirteen

All her life Claudia wanted a sister to share her hopes and dreams. When Marcus was born she smothered him with love. As he got older she would dress him in costumes from her dressing-up box. Sometimes he would be the queen and she would be the king but Claudia was always in charge instructing him in the finer art of court protocol. Marcus consistently rose to the occasion. He adored Claudia and followed her around. She soon forgot her desire for a sister.

When Marcus became ill she was sent away to live with her aunt Magdalena on the other side of Andorra. This distressed her as no one would discuss Marcus' illness or give her any information. Mama looked at her and at times would not speak to her or answer any questions about Marcus. Claudia felt responsible for his illness. This was because of her mother's changed attitude towards her. Claudia always knew that Marcus was the favourite sibling but it did not affect her because Marcus' love for her was apparent.

One day she found her aunt distraught, and on enquiry, learnt that one of Marcus' friends had died from mumps encephalitis. This information compounded her distress at the separation from her family and frightened her. She found it difficult to verbalise her feelings and her greatest fear was that Marcus had died or would die and no one would tell her. She cried herself to sleep that evening and she made a promise that if God spared Marcus' life, she would dedicate her own life in the service of others.

Marcus' recovery from mumps filled her with great joy. She was soon able to return to her family home. She felt a strange sense of calm. As they grew older and Claudia became aware that Marcus was unable to father children, her resolve to be of service to others became more intense. Her studies enveloped her and she excelled as an A student. She studied medicine at university and focused her energies on genetics, as her secret desire to have a sister now morphed into becoming an aunt.

Claudia was delighted when Marcus brought his girlfriend home for the first time. Marcia was everything that he had described. She was shy and sweet and did not speak much but stayed close to Marcus. Marcus had kept her a secret from the family but he confided in Claudia. He did not want his parents asking too many questions about the relationship in case it brought up the question of his infertility. He was self-conscious of the fact that he was infertile and did not want to be asked embarrassing questions by his mother. He had that when he was at university and he did not find it a pleasant experience.

He remembered meeting Marcia for the first time. He told his sister that he had seen the girl he was going to marry. Claudia was overjoyed. He returned to the car park early the following morning in the hope he would meet Marcia again. He was pleased when Marcia accepted his invitation to dinner.

As Claudia observed the closeness of their relationship, not only was she happy for her brother but she also found a friend to replace the sister she always wanted. Claudia noticed that although Papa embraced Marcia, Mama was reticent, but she never imagined her Mama would behave in that despicable way towards Marcia or indeed anyone. She was shocked and disturbed by the event that occurred in Marcus' flat. She was unable to associate the abuse with the mother she loved. It was difficult for her to separate her duty towards her mother and the intense love she felt for Marcus, Marcia and the baby at that time.

At first she was stunned into silence by her mother's behaviour and her aunt's acquiescence, but when Mama called for her to leave she knew that her allegiance lay with her brother and his wife. Claudia felt a sudden empathy with Marcia because she had no family. She could not leave her to cope on her own. In that moment she turned her attention to Marcus, Marcia and the baby without thinking of the repercussions.

When Marcia developed puerperal fever, Claudia worried about the possible outcome of the disease. It caused her anxiety, which she suppressed because Marcus became increasingly dependent on her, especially for interaction with Dr Jameson. The doctor was an affable person and time spent in his company allayed her fears. She felt he was a person of integrity who willingly interacted directly with his patients by making himself available. He epitomised the holistic approach to medicine to which she thought all doctors should aspire. His bedside manner and his availability to the family gave them confidence and engendered a feeling of trust and hope. He kept them informed of all developments and listened attentively to their queries. Whilst discussing in detail Marcia's illness, he explained carefully and in simple terms the legal aspects of Marcus Aurelius' birth and the possible outcomes.

Claudia fantasised that if the situation was different, he appeared to be the type of person she would love to be acquainted with. In fact she felt a deep desire to be closer to him, but knew that would be impossible as Dr Jameson was already married.

Chapter Fourteen

Tall, dark and slightly grey at the temples, Dr Jeremy James Jameson cut an imposing figure. His charming, engaging attitude created trust and confidence for his patients and their relatives. He loved his job and felt blessed to be in a position to give aid to so many people. Every baby he delivered filled him with immense joy. He revelled in the look of happiness and elation that the parents experienced, especially at the first-born.

He knew he wanted to be a doctor from an early age. His paternal grandfather and his father were both eminent doctors, and he was named after them. He remembered when he was aged three, his father took him to the hospital on Christmas Day. The nurses, doctors, patients and their relatives fussed over him. He observed how his father was treated with deferential respect and how the patients and staff were in awe of him.

It was at medical school that he met Julia. It was an immediate attraction. They gravitated towards each other and it was not long before they were planning their nuptials. Their wedding coincided with their graduation as doctors. Dr Jameson fiddled with his wedding ring as he recalled many memories, some painful and some gloriously happy. It was nearly five years now since Julia had been expecting their first child, but she was unaware. He felt shame and guilt that he was not more attentive towards her. The irony of it all. He gave a wry smile.

When he saw Claudia, it was the first time since his wife's death that he thought of a possible relationship with another woman. Her beauty and the professional way she conducted herself struck him. In fact, he made a conscious effort to maintain his professionalism. He observed that her ring finger was bare and wondered if she had any romantic involvement. These thoughts and his reaction to meeting Claudia were alien to him. They troubled him but he suppressed them. At subsequent meetings he exercised restraint, as he was aware that he was beginning to think of her as he once thought of Julia.

It was a shock to him when Dr Ellam presented his findings. Never in his years of practice had he encountered a case such as Marcia and Marcus. He felt responsible for doing the DNA test. He wondered how many other families were exposed to that situation without being aware. He thought about the long-term challenges that could result from being a human chimera. He made a decision to help the family resolve the conflict that surrounded Marcus Aurelius' birth.

His engagement with the family became pensive and pleasurable in lots of ways. Claudia was always present and she handled all Marcus' affairs with an efficiency that he admired. He observed her compassionate dealings with her brother, who seemed to be falling apart. He did not get involved but he felt empathy. He remembered when he was called by the hospital and told his wife was seriously ill. At the time he was unable to comprehend how that was possible. When she left him a few hours before she was perfectly well. The duty doctor refused to discuss her ailment and told him to come at once.

He made haste to the hospital and found Julia was in the operating theatre, with his colleagues desperately attempting to save her life. The theatre superintendent was awaiting his arrival and prevented him from entering. An undiagnosed ectopic pregnancy had ruptured with catastrophic consequences. He did not even get to say goodbye.

Dr Jameson shook his head as he recalled his inability to communicate the nagging grief that encompassed him. He was unable to work as he endeavoured to understand how both of them, especially him, an obstetrician and gynaecologist, could have missed Julia's pregnancy. He found it difficult to forgive himself and, as a result, blame followed him wherever he went.

He recognised in Marcus the same behaviour that haunted him. He also understood, from his own experience, why Marcus did not want to be kept informed. It was the fear of negative information plus the feeling of culpability. In short, he reflected that Marcus had an inability to process and balance the immediacy of Marcia's illness and his mother's response to Marcus Aurelius' birth.

Dr Jameson was always kind to his patients, but when he eventually returned to work he made an extra effort to ensure all his patients had optimum care and next of kin were informed about possible outcomes. He spent time listening to his patients' and their relatives' concerns in the gentlest of manner. At the hospital he worked long hours on his research. There was a reluctance to return home during waking hours, as the house held memories that reminded him of Julia's death rather than her life. As he pondered his work-life balance, the image of Claudia remained prominent in his thoughts.

The pending court case occupied his mind. He was called by the judiciary to explain the circumstance of Marcus Aurelius' birth. Dr Ellam was also called to give evidence in the specially convened court that was held in secret. The law lords greeted the evidence with some degree of alarm but Dr Ellam was able to describe, in graphic detail, the history of DNA profiling and the rare occasion that this particular case presented. They were mesmerised by his account of the stress and agony that some human chimeras had suffered, in other parts of the world, by their spouse, the law and the press, for being classed as *excluded* after DNA testing.

Dr Jameson and Dr Ellam left the proceedings after giving their evidence. It had been an exhausting time for them. The information that they had accrued and passed on in court was completely new learning for all those involved in the decision making process. Many questions were asked and countless hypotheses were advanced but, in the end, the law lords retired for their deliberation. The two doctors returned to the hospital to await the outcome of the case.

Chapter Fifteen

After a period of intense deliberation, it was fortuitous that the judiciary accepted the evidence provided by the hospital pertaining to Marcus Aurelius' birth. The emergency court dutifully agreed that Marcia was a chimera and her twin lived microscopically inside her body as DNA. A challenging process, simplified by evidence gleaned by Dr Ellam from documented cases worldwide. Input from Dr Jameson and Claudia provided substantial proof.

Marcia was enshrined in law as the non-biological, but birth mother of Marcus Aurelius. The courts further recommended that the parents formally adopt the baby and any subsequent children as a precaution. The results of the judiciary were greeted with adulation. Marcia and Marcus were spared the ordeal of being in court as the case was held in secret.

It was a momentous occasion for all concerned. Claudia used her expertise as a researcher to interact with doctors who had written research papers on blood dyscrasias. She was also able to speak directly to two chimera mothers in the USA. They had experienced enormous challenges in law to be recognised as mothers of their children. They were accused of fraud and deceit, and the courts threatened to send them to prison and foster their children.

Claudia found a new focus to add to her research. She collaborated with Dr Jameson and Dr Ellam as she gathered information to prepare the case for the hospital. A closeness developed between her and Dr Jameson, as they met frequently to discuss her findings and share with Dr Ellam.

Claudia had been thinking about her own fertility. This was a recent occurrence. During her research into Marcia's case, she discovered a high percentage of females that she interviewed found it difficult to conceive. She thought about her aunt, Magdalena, and the difficulty she experienced having children. She remembered as a teenager overhearing a conversation between Mama and her sister about Magdalena's infertility, and the extensive treatment that she needed to have children, plus the difficulty Mama herself had had conceiving. Claudia's mother was never forthcoming in discussing matters of an intimate nature with her daughter. This made it impossible for Claudia to ask her for information. As a result, Claudia made a decision to take pre-emptive action. She telephoned Dr Ellam for an appointment.

* * *

Claudia entered Dr Ellam's office and he greeted her with outstretched arms.

"Good morning, Claudia. It is good to see you. Thank you for all the hard work you did on that fascinating case. Marcus and Marcia must be proud of you. The hospital is indebted to you for your diligence."

"Good morning, William. It was exciting and enhanced my knowledge significantly with information I can now include in my research."

"Do sit down and tell me what is bothering you," demanded Dr Ellam.

Claudia hesitated, then said, "It's a personal matter that arose as a result of the research."

"I see. How can I help?" Dr Ellam nodded, and Claudia continued.

"It is to do with my family's history of infertility," Claudia said, and Dr Ellam interrupted her.

"It's alright Claudia. I have been expecting you. We can do an initial blood profile of your Anti-Mullerian Hormone and Follicle-Stimulating Hormone. We already have your DNA profile. The results are pretty quick and if you like, when they are ready, we can discuss them. I can refer you to a gynaecologist. I take it that you would rather not see Jeremy."

Claudia blushed and said, "How did you guess?"

"I suspected that you would want to examine your fertility profile, so I prepared forms to expedite the process. Go to see the phlebotomist. You do not need an appointment. I told her to expect you."

Claudia stood up.

"Thank you, William."

"No. Thank you, Claudia. Your input," he paused. "You did an amazing job that made our lives a lot easier. It was helpful to have a researcher on board."

Claudia smiled and thanked Dr Ellam again as she took her leave. She then went to the laboratory where a series of tests were completed. The following morning, Dr Ellam told Claudia that all her results were within normal limits.

* * *

It was late afternoon when Claudia went to see Dr Jameson. She knocked on his door.

"Come in."

As she entered Jeremy stood up.

"What a pleasant surprise. I was wondering if I would see you prior to your leaving."

Claudia smiled and said, "I couldn't leave without thanking you for all that you did for my family."

"Nonsense," said Dr Jameson. "You were the driving force behind much of our accomplishments. It was great to have you on board. I hope we will have the opportunity to work together again."

Claudia walked over to the oriel window and looked outside. Through the little copse of trees she observed the fountain and the flowerbeds in the distance. Jeremy followed and stood behind her.

"I cannot begin to describe my joy on becoming an auntie. All my life I wanted a sister, then Marcus brought Marcia home. When I first saw the baby my heart raced, but, when Mama was abusive to Marcia, words failed me. Marcia is such a sweet thing. I couldn't understand. Why? This whole episode has left me bereft. I know that I have to confront Mama when she arrives back in London but suddenly, I am afraid."

Jeremy placed one hand on her shoulder and said, "I will help if you wish."

Claudia turned and he drew her close and kissed her. She withdrew and bowed her head.

Jeremy stepped backwards saying, "I am sorry. I don't know what came over me. Do forgive me."

Claudia opened her mouth to speak but no words came.

Jeremy stepped back further, muttering. "I am sorry. I am so sorry. Please forgive me. I have grown fond of you and I am sad that you are leaving..."

"I am sad too," interrupted Claudia, "but we must both forget this incident. We must not see each other again. I will never come between a man and his wife no matter how fond I am of him."

With that, she turned and fled the room. Jeremy hesitated, stunned. He began to play with his wedding ring. Of course, Claudia would be unaware about his wife. He rushed out of the room but Claudia was nowhere to be seen. He returned to his office, packed his bags and left.

* * *

Claudia rushed out of the hospital and sought seclusion in the remembrance garden. She sat on the bench by the fountain, listening to the sounds of cascading water. She was shocked by what had happened. She desperately wanted to be with Jeremy but her moral compass did not allow her to be in a relationship with a married man. Thoughts raced through her head. How could she be so stupid? She blamed herself for going alone to his office. Claudia knew that she was attracted to him. If only she had met him on neutral ground to say goodbye. Was he a philanderer? A surge of pity for his wife and herself overwhelmed her and she began to cry. Claudia endeavoured to compose herself prior to going to the car park.

"Claudia. Claudia. Please. I must speak with you," she heard Dr Jameson shouting as he ran towards her.

She stopped, uncertain, and said, "Please don't. We have nothing to say to each other. I am going back to the flat now. You and I have nothing to discuss."

Claudia continued to walk away from him, but he followed her and said in a calming, controlled voice, "Claudia, my wife is dead. I wear my ring because my wife, Julia, gave it to me. Please. Please let me explain. I am sorry I offended you. I was as surprised as you were by my actions. Please forgive me."

Claudia stopped, turned, and then retraced her steps. She walked over to the bench and sat down. Jeremy followed and sat beside her. She stared into space, her thoughts muddled by what she had heard. She had no idea. Many scenarios raced through her mind. How did she die? How long ago? Is he telling the truth? Is he being honest? Can I trust him? She kept her counsel. As darkness fell, Jeremy broke the silence.

"Claudia. It's getting cold. You can't sit here all evening. Please can we go somewhere warm where we can talk? If you don't want to I will understand but you can't stay here in the cold."

Claudia looked at him, her face pale and tear-stained.

"Where can we go that is safe?"

"We can return to my office. It's warm there and I will get you some tea. I promise I will not cause you any more pain. I am so sorry."

Claudia acquiesced and they returned to his office.

* * *

Jeremy sat away from Claudia. He ordered hot drinks, which were imbibed with a sprinkling of polite conversation. He chose his words carefully and spoke in a quiet, controlled voice.

"Claudia. I want you to know that I never meant to hurt you. Please listen to what I have to say. It's about Julia. She was my wife. It is personal and private. I have never discussed the events of Julia's death with anyone but feel that I owe you an explanation after what occurred earlier."

Claudia interrupted and said, "I think I would have stayed if I knew that you weren't married. It shocked me to know that I was... well, you were married."

"I met Julia at medical school. The moment I saw her I only wanted to be with her. We were married for five years. One day, I got a phone call saying my wife was very seriously ill and I needed to come to the hospital at once. I arrived to find my colleagues desperately trying to save her life. She had a ruptured ectopic pregnancy and she died without me seeing her and saying goodbye. I blamed myself. Nothing could absolve me from the blame. You see, I am an obstetrician and gynaecologist. I did not know that Julia was pregnant. She had been complaining of abdominal pain and I presumed it was *female problems*. She trusted me. Julia trusted me. I failed her. If only I had listened and asked one of my colleagues to examine her. She would be alive today."

Jeremy held up his left hand and continued.

"Julia gave me this ring. It's the only tangible item of her that I have."

He paused. "It serves a dual purpose. It reminds me of her love and of my failure. That reminder allows me to listen to my patients and understand their fears. My inadequacies follow me wherever I go. I beg her to forgive me. Yes. I am married. I am married to a memory of a life I betrayed. When I saw you, it was the first time since Julia's death, that I felt the sensations I had when I first saw Julia."

Dr Jameson hesitated, and then added, "This is my life in a nutshell. I apologise again for hurting you. My hope is that we could be friends and that you will forgive me."

Claudia gave a half-smile and said, "There is nothing to forgive. I too am fond of you. It's very sad about your wife. Sometimes in life we blame ourselves for occurrences beyond our control. In some way I can empathise with you. I am devoted to Marcus. I blamed myself for his illness. When we were children, he succumbed to mumps and I did not. I believed that Mama wanted it to be me instead of him. She has always been obsessed with him. That thought lives with me, so I am always available for Marcus and that keeps my mother happy. I am sorry about your wife."

"Thank you Claudia. Can we remain friends and see each other?"

"Yes. I should like that but I must get back to the flat. I have to make arrangements for the family homecoming."

"Allow me to walk with you to the car park."

"Thank you."

They made their way to Claudia's car. Jeremy held the door as Claudia got in. "May I call you tomorrow? Perhaps we could have dinner?" Dr Jameson asked.

"Yes. I would like that," replied Claudia.

"Goodnight."

Jeremy watched as Claudia drove away. He went to his car. He sat there for some time thinking about the events that had occurred. He felt relief that finally he was able to talk to someone he trusted, about the burden of guilt he carried.

Claudia's drive back to Marcia and Marcus' home was preoccupied with the events that had occurred in Jeremy's office. Her reaction shocked her. The degree of emotions experienced, and the cathartic release that followed, took her by surprise. As she rehearsed the scene in her mind she was unsure of her response to the knowledge that Jeremy was a widower. Her overriding feeling was elation, as the possibility of a relationship with Jeremy filled her with joy. However, the demise of his wife troubled her. When she arrived at the flat the telephone was ringing. It was Marcus.

"Hello Claudia."

"Hi Marcus. Is everything alright?"

"I am not sure. Mama and Auntie are coming to London. They arrive tomorrow. Auntie telephoned and I said that you would collect them from the airport. I hope that was all right. I didn't want to leave Marcia." Marcus paused. "In truth, I didn't want to see Mama or Auntie."

"Oh Marcus. Of course I will collect them. I have to confront Mama before she is allowed to visit you, Marcia, and the baby. Don't worry. Mama will come only if I have her assurance that she will apologise and be respectful. I am sure I don't know what possessed her to behave in the way she did but I aim to find out."

"Claudia, you have been my strength. I don't know how I would have managed these difficult days without you."

"How are Marcia and my favourite nephew?"

Marcus laughed.

"They are both doing well. Marcia is looking forward to seeing you. She missed you today. She wants to speak to you. Hold on."

"Hello Claudia."

"Hello, Marcia. It is good to hear you. Sorry I missed you today, I was saying my goodbyes."

"Dr Jameson wants us to remain for a while longer to resolve any outstanding issues, but Marcus is worried about Mama's visit."

"I am collecting Mama and Auntie from their flight tomorrow. Don't worry. If Mama doesn't behave I will not bring her to see you and Marcus Aurelius when you return home."

"Thank you, Claudia. But I am looking forward to seeing Mama, especially when she holds the baby for the first time. She will be so happy."

* * *

It was nearing time for Marcus and Marcia to return home with the baby. Marcus was beginning to feel less pressured. His only challenge was dealing with his mother for the way she treated Marcia. He abdicated that responsibility to Claudia. His boss was exceptional in his understanding of Marcus' plight. A sabbatical was arranged so Marcus could adjust and look after his family. Marcia was given extended maternity leave.

After conversing with Claudia, Marcus left the room to say personal goodbyes to the staff. Marcia sat in silence, pondering motherhood. She never knew she was one half of a twin. Now, there was a reason for the intense feelings of isolation she felt as a child. It was now evident to her that she was always mourning the loss of her twin even though she was unaware of her existence.

Marcia smiled at the memories she had of Lucy, her imaginary friend, as she remembered her attempts at discussing Lucy with Sister Alyusia. It was only after she met Marcus that Lucy's closeness appeared to wane. On reflection, while she was unknowingly pregnant, Lucy seemed to be around but she did not attach any significance to her frequent appearances.

Marcia always welcomed the warmth of Lucy's presence. There was a profound feeling of loss and isolation without it. She remembered her childhood feelings of insecurity and she embraced Lucy's essence. The awareness of Lucy always created for her a safe and secure environment. Marcia felt loved.

Chapter Sixteen

Claudia drove to the airport to collect Maria, Magdalena and the twins. She was looking forward to seeing her mother but she was anxious. Claudia knew that a confrontation was necessary. She needed to address the issue of her mother's behaviour towards Marcia.

Marcus had confided in her that he was afraid to see his mother. He did not want to tell Mama how he felt about her treatment of Marcia and the consequences of her actions. He told Claudia that he was afraid because he was being forced to choose between Mama and his wife. He did not want to be forced to make that choice because if he did, it would mean he would never see his mother again. This was uppermost in his mind and was the cause of his anxiety.

Claudia was sympathetic. She knew how much her brother loved both his mother and his wife. She also knew that he would never leave Marcia. She assured Marcus that she would speak to their mother and gain her assurance that an apology to Marcia was forthcoming, otherwise Mama would not be allowed to see either Marcia or Marcus Aurelius and in addition loose contact with her son.

Claudia collected Maria, Magdalena and the twins from the terminal building at the airport and took them to their hotel. They were shown first to Magdalena's room that she would share with Andreas and Felix. She then accompanied Mama to her room. When they entered, Claudia stood with her back against the closed door as she observed her mother unpack. Mama then sat on a chair.

"Mama. Why did you behave in such a despicable manner towards Marcia?"

"Don't you speak to me in that tone of voice," Mama retorted.

"But, it was alright for you to be horrid to Marcia when she was obviously shocked at becoming a mother almost overnight," Claudia remarked.

"It's none of your business what I say or do. I don't have to explain my actions to you. Have you forgotten that I am your mother?" Mama replied sarcastically.

"Yes, you do have to explain yourself to me. And no, I haven't forgotten that you are my mother. You owe Marcia and Marcus an apology. Your behaviour was not what I expected of my mother. I am ashamed of you. I believe that you must have a reason for behaving in such an unseemly manner."

"How dare you? Who do you think you are to speak to me in this way? Just you remember. I am your mother and you have no right to speak to me this way."

"Well, I will not allow you to visit Marcia until I understand why you hate her. If you want to see Marcia you must apologise to her for your behaviour. If you don't apologise you will not be able to see Marcus or your grandson either. Is that what you want? I believe that this is more about you than Marcia. She is a sweet girl. In all the time I have known her she has been the best friend and kindest person I know. Even after you treated her so badly, all she wants is for you to be happy and meet your grandchild." Claudia paused, then continued in a controlled voice as her mother glared at her.

"Why do you hate her? Do you feel threatened by her? Is it because you wanted to replace Papa with Marcus and you see her as a threat?"

"How dare you accuse me? You don't know what you are talking about. How dare you speak to me in this way? Get out. Get out. Leave me alone!" Mama screamed.

"I am not going anywhere until I have an explanation for your behaviour. I cannot allow you to see Marcia and Marcus. You made them both ill with your abuse. Marcia almost died and Marcus is falling apart. He is torn between the love for his wife and his love for you. Mama, as a doctor, I cannot allow you to cause further distress to their family. The stress of being unplanned new parents and having Marcia in intensive care is not helpful when..."

Mama burst into tears.

"Shut up. Shut up. Do you hear? Just shut up." Mama covered her ears and screamed at Claudia.

"You don't know what you are talking about. No one knows. Only me. Papa never knew."

"Papa never knew what?" Claudia asked.

"I am sorry. You are right. It's not Marcia. It's me. I have been unable to sleep since that day in Marcus' flat. I am so ashamed of my behaviour. It is not Marcia. It is I. I am the one at fault."

Claudia walked over to her mother and said, "What is it Mama? What caused you to hate Marcia with such intensity?"

Mama looked at Claudia with tears streaming down her face. She clasped her arms across her chest and rocked backwards and forwards in the chair.

"You are my daughter but not my firstborn. Don't you see? We are a family but I have skeletons in my closet."

"No. No. No. Mama. Is it what I am thinking? Please say it isn't so. Please Mama, please, say it isn't so."

Mama bowed her head and muttered, "Yes Claudia. No one knows except me. You understand now why I disputed the baby's father. It was about me. Not Marcia."

Claudia covered her mouth.

"You mean Papa is not Marcus' father."

Mama collapsed in hysterical laughter. Through her tears she replied, "No, Claudia. Papa is Marcus' father."

"Then it's me... Oh no. It's me."

"No Claudia. Papa is your father."

"Then what?" said Claudia, perplexed.

Mama hesitated then said, "You see. I had an abortion when I was not yet fifteen. Not even my mother knew. Maybe now you will understand and forgive me."

Claudia remained silent, staring at her mother in disbelief as mama continued.

"Marcia is a devout Catholic. She was going to join The Convent prior to meeting Marcus. Every time I see Marcia's saintly face, I remember. You see," Mama paused, "Marcia is a constant reminder of my sins. One sin following another and never being able to repent."

Mama's tear-stained face was contorted with guilt and shame. She looked past Claudia with unseeing eyes. Claudia watched and listened with a sense of disbelief as Mama continued with her story, her voice scornful as she spoke.

"I have a tranche of secrets. My father, your grandfather, took away my innocence. He said unspeakable things would occur if ever I told anyone. He made me feel worthless and said no one would believe me. I was terrified of him. He arranged to take me to summer school but it was to the hospital for an abortion. I did go to summer school but I was a failure. When I returned home he would stare at me and I would remember, with fear, his promise.

"One day I came home from school. I let myself into the house as usual. I went upstairs to my bedroom. I did not expect him to be there. He was waiting for me. I screamed when I saw him and he grabbed me and covered my mouth with his hands. All at once I froze. My bag fell from my hand and my books scattered. His grip loosened then he slumped to the floor. He whined mournfully. I just stood transfixed and watched as he clutched his chest and begged for help until he could beg no more."

"I picked up my books, one by one, retraced my steps and stayed in the kitchen until my mother returned home. She found him crumpled on the floor by the door to my bedroom. Dead. Her screams echoed around the house. I ran upstairs and pretended to be shocked and distressed. I went through the motions of a grieving daughter, secretly hating all the rituals. My whole life after that became a pretence, because now only I knew my secret and I learned not to be afraid anymore."

Claudia listened with a growing sense of disbelief and panic as her mother continued.

"When I met Papa, he was a devout Catholic. I too went to church religiously, but at confession, never told the priest of my unforgivable sins. You see, my whole life has been a lie. Papa was a loving husband. He never once made demands on me for his conjugal rights. It was three years before our marriage was consummated. He loved me and took care of me. I never told him or my mother what happened to me as a child. I felt shame, guilt and fear. I still do. So you see, Marcia unwittingly brought my buried past to life. Marcia is shy and sweet. Every time I see her or hear her name mentioned I am reminded of my lost childhood, my unforgivable sins, and the fact that I let my father die. I hated my father with uncontrollable venom and that is the essence of my hatred towards Marcia. It is her innocence that I despise, not her. So you are right, Claudia. It is all about me, not Marcia. Now you know my story maybe you will understand and forgive me."

Claudia's gaze was fixed on her mother. She remained speechless. Her mouth opened but no words came out.

Mama paused, bowed her head and whispered, "Please, for my sake, do not repeat what I have told you. I will apologise to Marcia and Marcus. I will ask their forgiveness, but they must never know the truth. No one must know the truth. Promise me. Promise me. I always knew it was Marcus' baby. I know that Marcia would never be unfaithful to him, but when I saw her holding the baby, the hatred that I had internalised for my father was vented on the unsuspecting girl. When Marcus telephoned about the birth I thought of the baby I had killed and the circumstances of the pregnancy. My anger was intense. I used words that left me feeling humiliated yet unable to right the wrongs. I am sorry. I am so sorry that I caused pain and suffering to my family. Please find it in your heart to forgive me. Do you think Marcus and Marcia will ever forgive me?"

Claudia continued looking at her mother in disbelief. Tears trailed down her cheeks. Her knees buckled and slowly she slid onto the floor. She sat there and stared at her mother. Her mother's past was now her present and it was Claudia who now felt fear.

Her mother's confession was unexpected and frightening. Her mother's words did not compare with the person she knew as Mama. Claudia found it difficult to comprehend and process the information that she had just heard. She remained sitting on the floor. Her gaze fixed on her mother. Her mind numbed. She was unable to respond.

Chapter Seventeen

Claudia arranged a surprise homecoming for Marcus Aurelius. She told Mama and Auntie to remain at the hotel with Andreas and Felix. She invited Jeremy to help her prepare the flat with balloons and bunting. He eagerly accepted. Claudia also employed a catering firm to provide refreshments. The priest was also summoned to bless the flat and perform a service of thanksgiving.

Jeremy, the priest and guests remained in the flat while Claudia collected her mother, aunt and the twins from the hotel. They were unaware of the planned celebrations. The children became excited at the prospect of seeing the baby again. Mama and auntie were surprised at the reception Claudia had prepared. Mama was especially pleased to meet Dr Jameson.

Everyone was present when Marcia and Marcus arrived home with the baby. Claudia opened the door and said, "It's great to have you home."

Marcus was holding Marcus Aurelius and before they could respond, everyone shouted, "Welcome Home. Congratulations, Marcia."

Marcia and Marcus were thrilled at the unexpected reception they received. Their faces were alive with joy. Mama walked over to Marcia.

"I apologise for the harsh words I said to you. I am profoundly sorry for my behaviour. I cannot begin to tell you how ashamed I feel. Please. Please find it in your heart to forgive me."

Marcia embraced Mama as Marcus and Claudia looked on. Everyone else was focused on the baby.

"I understand. We were all shocked at the news. I was overwhelmed and terrified, especially as Marcus was away. I felt helpless. It never occurred to me to telephone Claudia. All I could think of was Marcus and what he would say when he found out that I had a baby," Marcia said in a subdued voice.

Mama wiped tears from her eyes and looked apologetically at Marcia.

"Marcia, may I please hold the baby?"

Marcia took the baby from Marcus. She placed him in Mama's arms and said, "Mama, may I present Marcus Aurelius Dos Santos, your grandchild."

Everyone applauded. Mama held her grandson close. Her face beamed with pride as she said, "If only Papa was here. I would be able to share my happiness with him. Marcus Aurelius looks just like Marcus with his crop of black curls."

Laughter rippled around the room. Marcus walked over to Marcia. She turned, looked at him, and smiling said, "Now Mama has the happiness she always wanted."

Acknowledgements

This book is dedicated to Dr Bahaa Abdelmegid, a poet, author, translator, and a very dear friend, who returned to his heavenly home on Sunday 13 December 2020. He was a Lecturer in Poetry and Director of the International and Cooperation Office at the Ain Shams University, Cairo, Egypt.

Dr Bahaa translated some of my poems into Arabic. Our sharing of poetry and literary fiction formed a great bond of mutual support between us. I will miss the conversations with him and his beloved wife.

Sincere thanks to Stephen and Antony for their unstinting support.

Thank you to Daniel Heijink for his front cover design which made my vision a reality.

I am also grateful to Dr J D Ballam, Director of the Creative Writing Diploma at the University of Oxford, for his continuing support and encouragement.

With gratitude to His Excellency Professor Desmond Ian Gosford Hall for his loving kindness and support of my work.

Finally, thank you to Kash Ali and all at Hansib Publications for their understanding approach and valuable assistance in the publication of my book.